A MIDSUMMER'S
NIGHTMARE

A MIDSUMMER'S NIGHT

MARE

a novel by Kody Keplinger

poppy

LITTLE, BROWN AND COMPANY
New York Boston

Copyright © 2012 by Kody Keplinger

Poppy

Hachette Book Group
237 Park Avenue, New York, NY 10017
For more of your favorite novels, visit www.pickapoppy.com

Poppy is an imprint of Little, Brown and Company.
The Poppy name and logo are trademarks of Hachette Book Group, Inc.

The publisher is not responsible for websites (or their content) that are not owned by the publisher.

First Edition: June 2012

Library of Congress Cataloging-in-Publication Data

Keplinger, Kody.
A midsummer's nightmare / by Kody Keplinger. — 1st ed.
    p. cm.
Summary: Suffering a hangover from a graduation party, eighteen-year-old Whitley is blindsided by the news that her father has moved into a house with his fiancée, her thirteen-year-old daughter Bailey, and her son Nathan, in whose bed Whitley had awakened that morning.
    ISBN 978-0-316-08422-2
    [1. Conduct of life—Fiction. 2. Fathers and daughters—Fiction.
3. Remarriage—Fiction. 4. Family problems—Fiction. 5. Illinois—
Fiction.] I. Title.
    PZ7.K439Mid 2012
    [Fic]—dc23   2011026949

10 9 8 7 6 5 4 3 2 1

RRD-C

Printed in the United States of America

For my mom and dad.
Thank you for never letting me feel like I was alone.
I love you both so much.

1

Hangovers are a bitch.

I've known this for years, since I was, like, fourteen and went to my first kegger, but the headache I woke up with the morning after graduation was the worst I'd *ever* experienced. And that says a lot. I mean, it was *throbbing.* I felt like someone had beaten me over the head with a freaking baseball bat. And God only knew, maybe someone had. I'd been so wasted that night I probably wouldn't have cared. I may have even found it funny at the time. Everything was funny after a few shots of tequila.

I groaned and pulled the blanket over my face, shielding my eyes from the sunlight that filtered through the window over my head. Why did it have to be so goddamn bright?

"Don't be dramatic. I'm not *that* ugly," a deep, groggy voice murmured beside me.

Shit.

Suddenly, I felt nauseous for reasons that had nothing to do with the amount of alcohol in my system.

I clenched my eyes shut, trying to remember what the hell I'd done last night. I'd danced with some people, played Quarters for a while, taken a few shots...*more* than a few shots. But, hey, it was a graduation party. Getting smashed was pretty much a requirement. I forced myself to think past the alcohol buzz and the thudding bass of the stereo, trying to remember where I'd been when I finally passed out.

And there it was.

At some point, after getting entirely shitfaced, I'd made out with some guy I didn't know — I graduated with almost a thousand kids, so I partied with a lot of strangers that night — and then I dragged him into one of the house's bedrooms. But everything after that was a blur. One thing I was sure of, though. I'd definitely had sex with him.

Goddamn it. Had I really been that drunk?

I opened my eyes and rolled onto my side. At this point, I just hoped he was cute. And he was...or he would have been if he hadn't looked so crappy. His brown eyes, staring at me from a few inches away, had deep lines under them, and his dark hair was a mess. Or maybe that was just the way he wore it. That was the style lately, for some reason.

Then again, I was sure I didn't look too hot at that moment, either. My hair, which had been totally awesome for graduation, was probably ratty from yesterday's hairspray, and I was sure my eyes were bloodshot and my makeup must have been runny and gross.

Like I said, hangovers are a bitch.

"Hi," the guy mumbled, rubbing his eyes. "Did you sleep okay?"

"Um...sure."

As if this whole situation weren't awkward enough, he was going to talk to me. I wished he'd just pretend to be asleep so I could sneak out in peace.

I sighed and pushed the blankets off me. The sunlight was killing my eyes. I had to squint as I stumbled around the room, gathering my clothes from the floor. I nearly fell over at least twice before I was dressed. Judging by the way everything was scattered, we'd had a pretty crazy night.

Good for me, I guess.

"Hey, um..." Christ, I couldn't even remember the dude's name. Had he ever told it to me? I cleared my throat and started again. "Do you think anyone will catch me if I go through the front door, or should I climb out the window? How are you leaving?"

"I'm not. This is my house."

So I'd screwed the host. I hadn't seen that one coming. The address was scribbled on every senior's hand yesterday, and I'd never thought to ask who lived in the place. A party was a party. Didn't matter who threw it.

"Or it used to be...Anyway, you won't get caught," he added, pushing himself up on the pillows. "Mom's not here. She and my sister had to leave town before graduation to

3

meet the movers. That's why I offered to have the party here. Partly for graduation, and partly as a going-away celebration."

"Okay, okay." I just needed a yes or no, not his whole life story. I grabbed my purse off the dresser. "So I'll use the front door. No big deal."

"Hey. Hold on a sec." He sat up straight, letting the covers fall away from his bare chest.

Yeah. He was definitely hot. Good body. I vaguely remembered telling him that, too. A tiny memory trickled into my consciousness: me giggling, poking him in the chest just after I'd pulled his shirt over his head. "Nice muscles you've got there, stud." He'd laughed and kissed me. He'd been a good kisser.

That was the most I could recall at the moment, though.

"Can I get your number?" he asked, running a hand through his sloppy brown hair. "So I can, you know, give you a call sometime."

Oh, God, was he serious?

Not that I had a whole lot of experience with one-night stands — I didn't, really; I mean, I could count the number of boys I'd slept with on one hand. But I had fooled around with a lot of guys while drunk, and most of them had the good sense not to try to keep in touch after. It was better for both of us if we just went on with our lives, pretending like the whole thing had never happened.

Apparently this dude — why couldn't I remember his name? — didn't feel the same way.

"Listen," I said, looking away from him as I pulled out the

4

condom wrapper that had managed to get tangled inside my shirt. "We just graduated, and after this summer we're off to college. So what's the point of staying in contact, really?" Ugh. Poor guy. I couldn't even let him down easy. This hangover was so bad. I met his eyes again, knowing I needed to get this over with so I could get out of there. "I think we should leave things where they are and, you know, never ever see each other again."

"So...you don't want to give me your number?"

"Not really. No."

He blew air out of his mouth in a rush. "Ouch. That's kind of harsh."

Maybe, but he was better off. It wasn't as if someone like me would have made a good girlfriend anyway. I was just some drunken hookup. That's all I'd ever been.

"Look, you're moving, right? I'm sure tons of girls in your new town will totally go for the slouchy pretty-boy thing you've got going on. You won't even remember last night in a week.... I barely remember already." I shrugged and slung my purse over my shoulder, one hand against the wall to keep me stable. "So, nice party. I had a good time. I, um, *won't* see you around."

"Whitley?" he called after me.

But I was already out of the bedroom and weaving unsteadily down the hall. I needed to get out of there. Fast. Not only was I ready to get away from Mr. Clingy, but I also really had to get home. Mom was waiting for me, and I had a shitload of packing to do before Dad showed up in his SUV the next day.

I reached the end of the hall and found the living room completely trashed. Beer cans and half-empty bags of chips had been tossed all over the floor. A recliner and an end table, the only pieces of furniture (I guess the rest had already been sent to his new place), were overturned. A couple stragglers remained passed out on the floor. I felt a little bad for whatshisname. He had a real mess to clean up. I was *so* glad not to be him.

That's what he got for volunteering to host a graduation bash, though.

I tripped over the garbage on my way to the front door, wincing when the light hit my eyes. My head hurt like hell, but at least I wasn't puking. After four years of going to high school keggers — and crashing the occasional frat party — I'd learned to hold my alcohol pretty well. Better than a lot of girls my age, anyway. Most of the girls I saw at parties were kissing the toilet after a couple bottles of Smirnoff Ice, then had to be carried out by their football player boyfriends. Babies.

With a sigh, I dug my cell phone out of my purse and dialed the number to the cab company. I seriously hoped I wouldn't get a chatty driver. If he said more than five words to me, I wasn't going to tip.

Mom was sitting at the kitchen table when I got home, eating frozen waffles in her housecoat and watching *Good Morning America*. She looked up when I walked through the door, the syrup bottle in her hand.

"Hey, Whitley," she said. "How was the rest of your night?"

"Good," I mumbled, going straight for the fridge. My mouth was unbelievably dry. "Sorry I didn't call."

"Oh, that's fine. I figured you were staying over at Nola's."

I grabbed a bottle of Gatorade, not bothering to inform my mother that Nola and I hadn't spoken since ninth grade. For a second, I wondered whether she'd notice if I did a line of coke on the table right in front of her. I doubted it.

"Trace sent you something," she said as I sat down in the chair beside her, clutching some Saltines for good measure and positioning myself to see the TV, which was on the counter across from us. She doused her waffles in syrup and pushed the bottle to the side. "I put it on your bed."

"Thanks."

We sat in silence for a long moment before Mom finally asked, "So, are you excited about graduating?"

She kept staring at the TV, watching as the national weather guy moved on from our part of the country and pointed at Florida, informing us that it was sunny — no shit, Sherlock. I got the feeling Mom didn't really give a damn about the answer. It was just one of those questions you ask because it makes you a crappy parent if you don't.

"Not really," I said, twisting the cap on the Gatorade and taking a big gulp. "Graduating isn't a big deal. It'll be nice to start college, though. Dad loved UK. Hopefully he can help me pick a goddamn major."

"Language, Whitley," she warned. "And, honey, be careful about taking your father's advice on this stuff. He can't even make smart life choices for himself, let alone help you make yours."

I scowled at her before taking another drink. Six years after the divorce, and she still slammed Dad at every opportunity. You'd think she'd be over it by now.

"I don't see anything wrong with how Dad lives," I told her.

"Please." She laughed bitterly. "In that trashy condo? Jumping from girlfriend to girlfriend? Forty-eight years old and still hasn't grown up at all. He can't even make enough time to see his own daughter more than once a year."

That's your fault, I thought. I stood up and tossed my Gatorade bottle in the trash, mumbling, "I'm going to lie down. Headache."

"All right, honey." Mom speared a bite of waffle with her fork. "I hope you get to feeling better. And don't forget to pack. Your father will be here to pick you up at noon tomorrow.... But you know how punctual he is." I didn't listen closely to the rest of her tirade.

I was halfway inside my bedroom before she finally shut up. When it came to Dad, my mother never knew when to just leave it alone. Everything about him annoyed her now: the way he dressed, the way he drove; she even said that the sound of his laugh made her cringe. She couldn't see how alike my father and I were, totally oblivious to the fact that some of the traits she loathed in him were part of me, too.

The worst part, though, was that Dad never said a bad word about her. She didn't know it, or she was too bitter to see, but Dad still cared about her feelings. That was the reason he'd said no when I'd asked to live with him four years ago — he said it would break Mom's heart if I moved out.

I never told Mom I'd asked Dad that. But over the years that followed, I became more and more certain that he was wrong. She wouldn't have even noticed if I left. She could bitch to a houseplant just as well as she could to me.

With my head hurting even worse, I yanked the curtains closed to block out any trace of sunlight and fell onto my bed, burying my face in the pillow with a groan.

I felt something stiff and crinkly under my stomach and sighed. The room had finally stopped spinning now that I was lying down, and sitting up seemed like a bad idea. Moving as little as possible, I reached beneath me and pulled out the offending object, holding it up to examine it. It was the thing Trace had sent me. A blue envelope with my name written across it with a pretty pink gel pen. Emily's doing, for sure. My brother's penmanship was shit.

With slow, unsteady movements, I opened the envelope and pulled out the card inside. YOU'VE COME A LONG WAY, the cover said. What a cliché. Inside, though, my brother had crossed out all the cheesy poem crap and written his own message. Of course, since Trace wrote it himself in his sloppy boy handwriting, it took me a few minutes to decipher.

hey kid—
so proud of you. so is emily. we wish we could have been
there, but here's a fat check to make up for it but
don't go spending it all on booze. call you soon.

Love, the best big brother ever
and Emily and Marie, too

I smiled. It was a mark of how much I loved my big
brother that I found his lack of punctuation and proper gram-
mar endearing.

Emily and Trace had been married for about two years.
They met when Trace got his job as the assistant to some talent agent out in Los Angeles. Emily was an actress — which
means she was a waitress — who was originally sleeping with
Trace's boss, trying to get parts. But then she met Trace, and
he claims it was love at first sight.

Normally, if someone told me that, I'd gag, but I bought
Trace's story. After they met, Emily dumped agent-man (she
wasn't getting any gigs anyway) and started dating my
brother. I figured that would be a conflict of interest with
Trace's job or something, but I guess that kind of crazy stuff
happens all the time in Hollywood because he was still working for the guy. He even got promoted after that. And Emily
had Marie, their daughter, just last month.

That was why Trace hadn't made it to my graduation.
Marie was too little to fly, and Trace didn't want to leave
Emily at home with the baby by herself.

I didn't blame him. He had a lot going on. And picking up and flying all the way out here for just one night would have been stupid. I mean, Dad hadn't even been able to make it because of work, and he lived within driving distance. It was no big deal. The ceremony was dumb anyway.

But it would have been nice to see Trace.

Next year, I thought, putting away the card and check he'd sent before curling up on my side and closing my eyes to fight off the headache. *Dad and I will fly out to California together during his vacation. No work, no Mom driving us crazy. It'll be great. Next year...*

And with that thought, I drifted off to sleep.

2

After the divorce, my mother insisted on moving as far from Dad as possible. I think she was shooting for California or Hawaii or something, but instead we wound up only two hundred and fifty miles away, just far enough so our antenna didn't pick up Channel 34.

My dad was this hotshot news anchor. He was, like, the most popular television personality in the tristate area or something. Channel 34 had the lowest ratings of all the local networks before they hired Greg Johnson to do the morning news. And everyone fell in love with him. Women wanted to date him, and men wanted to go fishing with him. Suddenly, Channel 34 was the most popular station in the area.

So, naturally, my mother wanted to move to a place where no one had ever heard of my dad. Even if that meant I was living far away from him, too.

At twelve, I was already old enough to realize how selfish my mother was being.

She moved us to a city four and a half hours from Dad — all the way to fucking Indiana — yet she had the nerve to bitch about how he didn't spend enough time with me. For God's sake, it wasn't his fault that she wasn't mature enough to live in the same state as her ex or that he had a job that took up a lot of his time, even weekends. Because of her, any traditional custody agreement just wasn't feasible. So Dad and I worked out a more convenient system.

I'd spent every summer for the last six years at my dad's condo. He lived only a few miles from Kentucky Lake, so I wasted most of the hot days stretched out on a towel, getting a tan on the beach. At night, Dad would fire up the grill, and last year he'd even mixed us a few drinks, making me promise Mom wouldn't find out. Sometimes his girlfriend — whoever she was that month — would come over, but he'd never let her stay long. The summer was our time. Our time to make up for the months spent apart.

And this was the last summer before college. I imagined sitting on the beach with Dad, talking about his days at University of Kentucky — where I'd be starting in September — him telling me the crazy stories from his fraternity days while we drank together. Maybe he'd even help me figure out what to major in when I got to UK. Mom said I should focus on business, but Dad knew me better than she did. That could be our project for the summer, deciding what I should do for the rest of my life.

When my dad pulled up the following afternoon, I didn't even wait for him to get out of the car before running off the front porch to meet him. I tossed my duffel bag into the back of his SUV, eager to hit the road and get our summer started. He was sitting in the driver's seat, talking to somebody on his cell phone and pretending he didn't notice Mom watching him from the front window of the house.

She'd never come outside when Dad was here. She'd swear she wanted nothing to do with him, but I always saw her watching.

"Ready to go, munchkin?" Dad asked, shutting his cell phone and plugging it into the car charger.

"Uh-huh." I slammed the SUV's door.

"Did you tell your mom good-bye?"

"Yeah," I muttered, climbing into the front seat. "Let's just get out of here."

"First put on your seat belt."

"Fine." I sighed, pulling the belt across me.

"Don't act so casual about it." He revved the engine. "We just aired a special report over at the station about the death rate for car accidents, and it's unreal the difference that little lap belt will make."

"Whatever."

Dad chuckled. "I don't know what I'm going to do with you, munchkin," he said, already backing out of my driveway.

I turned, thinking I might at least wave good-bye to Mom, but she wasn't at the window anymore. The blinds were shut. I wondered if she'd gone back to bed, if she'd stay

14

there for days the way she did for the first couple years after the divorce.

The sick part was that she's the one who left Dad. I think part of her assumed he'd chase after her or beg her not to go. But he didn't. After two months of separation, he sent her divorce papers, already signed. I didn't blame him. They fought all the time about stupid stuff. I was sure that was why Trace moved across the country after graduation — to get away from the drama. I was probably the only twelve-year-old to ever be relieved that her parents were getting divorced.

I was less relieved, however, when I realized this meant I had to live with my mom full-time. The first two years were the worst. When she wasn't depressed, she was angry. She was still angry now.

"Sorry I couldn't make it to your graduation," Dad was saying as we swerved through lunch-hour traffic. "I wanted to be there, but with my work schedule, it just wasn't possible."

"It's cool," I said, watching as the tall buildings of the city zoomed past the windows. "Graduation's nothing special anyway. It's actually really boring. But Mom recorded the ceremony on my digital camera so I could send it to Trace. If you want, I can load the file onto your computer and show you the footage once we get to the condo."

"Right...about the condo, munchkin...I have some news."

"What?" I turned to look at him, a little nervous as I remembered the beloved condo with its bright retro paintings and squeaky floorboards.

"It's really not a big deal," he said. "Nothing to get worked up about."

"Ugh. You don't have ants again, do you? I keep saying that you need to get a real exterminator in there instead of trying to do everything yourself."

"No, it's not ants," he said. "And I don't think we'll have to worry about those pests again because . . . well, I moved."

"Moved?" I repeated. "You mean, like, to a new house?"

"That's what I mean."

I stared at him, shocked. "But . . . you loved that condo. Why would you move? Did you want a place closer to the lake or something?"

"No, it wasn't about the beach."

"Then why give up the condo?" I asked. "If you're not going closer to the lake, there's no reason to live in Millerton."

"Well, I agree. But that's just it. I'm not living in Millerton."

"What? Really? But you've always lived in Millerton. You grew up there — *I* grew up there. Why would you leave?"

"You'll see when we get to Hamilton. You'll love it there, munchkin," he assured me. "It's a nice little neighborhood. Great surroundings. Wonderful people. You'll love spending your summer there, I promise. It's even better than Millerton."

Hamilton was a hellhole.

I discovered this three and a half hours later, after listening to every song on my iPod multiple times. I'd spent the drive giving Dad the silent treatment, annoyed that he hadn't warned me about this move. He'd always had a bad habit of springing things on me, like new girlfriends (those never lasted long enough to matter, though) or remodeling the condo. But never anything as drastic as moving to a new town.

A new, crappy town.

I was just thinking that I needed to get on iTunes to download some music when Dad's SUV rumbled past the WELCOME TO HAMILTON! sign. As soon as I saw that exclamation mark, I knew I was doomed. It only got worse as we drove farther into town.

Suburbs.

One stoplight.

A population of less than a thousand.

And definitely, *definitely* no beach. In fact, Dad's new house was on the opposite side of Channel 34's viewing area, which put us more than a hundred miles from the lake.

"Great," I muttered, watching out the window as white picket fence after white picket fence zoomed past. "So much for spending the summer in a bikini."

"Hey, don't get upset just yet, munchkin." He reached over to pat me on the knee.

Millerton had been twice the size of this place. It wasn't really a city, but there was a mall, at least, and all the houses didn't look exactly alike. There had been some diversity, some color. There were skate parks and weekend mini-golf places. And sometimes Dad took me to the go-kart track in the summer.

Unless they were hidden in the middle of a cornfield that separated the tiny neighborhoods, I doubted Hamilton had any of those things.

As we drove through the town, I spotted a library, a grocery store, a bank, and absolutely nothing fun to do.

"I'm going to be so pale when I start college," I whined.

"You'll still get a tan. We already have a pool."

"*We?*" I repeated. "Who's *we*? You mean you and me?"

"Actually..." Dad cleared his throat. "That's the second part of the surprise."

"Second part?"

We pulled into a driveway. The house we faced was pretty big, with a perfect, well-kept yard and neat little shutters on the windows. The part that caught my attention, though, was the woman standing on the front porch. She was tall, blond, and wearing super-high high heels.

"Dad," I said. "Who is that?"

He cut the engine and pushed open his door. "Sylvia!" he called out in his deep, booming voice. "Honey, I'm home!"

"*Honey?*" I frowned and climbed out of the SUV.

The woman was already jogging down the sidewalk, which I had to admit was impressive in those heels. Instead of running toward my father, she steered in the other direction and landed right next to me, reaching out and wrapping her arms around me in a tight hug before I could stop her. Thank God it was a quick one. When she stepped back, she was smiling at me like some kind of lunatic.

"Oh, Whitley," she said with a sigh, brushing blond hair

18

out of her heart-shaped face. "It is so nice to finally meet you. You are just so, so beautiful. Your dad's pictures don't do you justice at all."

"Uh, thanks…" I glanced over at Dad, who was making his way around the SUV, coming toward us. Then I looked back at this crazy woman. "Sorry, but who the hell are you?"

She looked taken aback for a minute before my father sidled up beside her, slipping his long arm around her shoulders. "This is Sylvia. My fiancée."

3

Once we were inside, I got the full story.

Sylvia Caulfield was a lawyer from Indiana. She and Dad had met last September when Dad was doing a story on Land Between the Lakes, a national recreation area near his condo, and Sylvia was there, visiting the park with a friend from college. Dad asked her for an interview about her experience at the park, and she asked for his phone number. Not long after that, they were crazy in love.

The story made me nauseous.

"We mostly exchanged e-mails and phone calls for a few months," Sylvia explained as she poured herself a mug of coffee in the house's cheerful kitchen. The pastel blues and greens were in direct contrast to my mood — four hours into vacation and already everything was ruined, and I had the strong urge to strangle my father and his bride-to-be.

"You sure you don't want a cup of coffee, Whitley?"

I shook my head. She had already offered me one, but I'd refused. I hated coffee with a passion. The smell alone was horrible.

"Well, anyway... Neither of us expected a long-distance relationship to work out. Especially me, I think. I hadn't dated since my first husband passed away from a heart attack a few years ago. This was so new to me. I was sure we'd break up before Christmas."

"Did you really think I'd let you get away that easy?" Dad asked, kissing her on the cheek. "I'm not *that* stupid."

She blushed and giggled.

I couldn't believe I was seeing this. It was like a bad made-for-TV movie. Poor little widow meets successful local celebrity. Then it's all flowers and sunshine in suburbia. Ew.

And it was so unlike Dad. After he and Mom split, my father had turned into a real flirt, which was, you know, pretty normal for a semifamous bachelor. Every summer when I came to visit he had a new twentysomething bombshell following him like a lost puppy. They always had names like Heather or Nikki, and they spent most of their time in way-too-revealing bikinis, lying on the beach and reading *Vogue*.

Sylvia wasn't one of those girls, though. In fact, the only thing she had in common with any of them was her hair color, but my father had always preferred blonds. Other than that, she was a total one-eighty from the usual bimbos. For one, she had a real job, whereas all the others had been

21

waitresses or retail clerks. And she was close to his age, too. So not his type.

What kind of spell did this chick have him under?

And how the hell could he not tell me about her?

"But we made it past Christmas," she said, sitting across from me at the kitchen table. I wrinkled my nose as the smell from her mug wafted my way. "Finally, we realized we just couldn't stand being apart for so long. Because, of course, your dad couldn't travel to see me with his work, and I don't get out-of-state cases that often."

"So I asked her to move in with me," Dad said.

"And I said no." Sylvia laughed. "I just couldn't live in that condo."

I scowled. I hated the way she said it. *That condo.* Like it was a bad place. Didn't she know that *that condo* had been a home to me? More of a home than Mom's house in Indiana ever had been.

"So we negotiated," Dad continued, either not seeing or choosing to ignore the glare I was giving them both. "I realized I wanted to marry her, but Sylvia wanted to live in a family community. She'd been in the city for too long, and she was right — that condo was just too *young* for me. It was a bachelor pad, and I wanted a real home. Plus, I was driving more than an hour to get to the station every morning. With that kind of trip twice a day, the money I was paying for gas was really ridiculous."

"And my sister lives here in Hamilton." Sylvia took a sip of her coffee, beaming at me over the top of the mug.

"We both knew that this was the perfect place for us. We

22

got engaged last month, and we finally moved everything in last night."

I looked at Dad, silently asking for a better explanation. Why? Why had he let this woman convince him to move out of the condo and into this place? Who was she to make him change? I kept hoping he'd burst out laughing and shout, *Got you! You really fell for it, munchkin.* But he didn't, and that pissed me off even more.

"I got an Illinois license to practice law, moved to a new firm — one closer — and now your dad is closer to his work, too," Sylvia was saying. "It's only thirty minutes to the station from here. And we both just love this little town. It's lovely, isn't it?"

"Sure," I muttered.

I'd been there for twenty minutes and already hated Hamilton. I never thought I'd say this, but I would have rather been back in Indiana. The city would have been better than this place. Dealing with Mom would have been better than dealing with this little surprise.

I couldn't believe Sylvia had talked Dad into moving here. Hamilton so wasn't his style. Dad liked bizarre pink flamingos and horseshoe pits in his yard. Not picket fences and cliché little gardens. At the condo, he had these crazy retro paintings and posters in trippy colors hanging from the walls. I think there was even a Velvet Elvis in his bedroom. But there was nothing like that in this house. Floral wallpaper. Watercolor art. Nothing with real personality. It was all generic and uniform.

I wanted to go back to the condo. Back home.

Sylvia got to her feet as the sound of the front door opening caught all of our attention. "That must be the kids," she said, hurrying into the living room.

I turned to Dad, stunned. "Kids?"

"Oh, yeah," Dad said, moving to sit in the chair next to mine. "Sylvia has two children."

I didn't say anything. I was shaking. Pissed, confused, overwhelmed. Mostly pissed, though. How dare this woman barge into our lives and change everything. How dare Dad *let her*! How could he just let this woman talk him into moving? How could he do it and not tell me?

"You okay, munchkin?" He brushed my long chestnut hair out of my face.

"It's kind of a lot to take in, Dad."

"I know," he said. "I'm sorry. But I really think you'll love them. The kids are great, and they're teenagers like you. And Sylvia's wonderful, isn't she?"

I didn't answer.

"Come on," he said, standing up and pulling me to my feet beside him. "The kids just got back from the grocery store, and I know they're dying to meet you."

So they knew about me? I wasn't warned about any of this, but Sylvia's little brats were totally prepared? I knew Dad wasn't much of a phone talker, but he couldn't even spare a few minutes to say, "Oh, hey, I'm getting married and moving to Illinois!"

I hadn't even been given a chance to say good-bye to the

condo. To the chilly wood floor I used to sprawl across on hot days. To the shower curtain decorated with multicolored fish and one random mermaid. To the goddamn Velvet Elvis. It was like I had no part of it. Like it had never been mine.

Well, this house wasn't mine, either. Maybe it was home to Sylvia and her spawn and even Dad — but it would never be home to me.

Before Dad and I could leave the kitchen, Sylvia's voice came through the dining room, her heels clicking across the tile as she headed toward the archway.

"Thanks for doing the grocery shopping," she was saying. "Greg and Whitley arrived a few minutes ago. Come in here and I'll introduce you guys." She smiled at me when she entered the kitchen, a plastic shopping bag dangling from her hand. "Nathan and Bailey are excited to meet you," she told me.

A second later a short blond girl appeared in the doorway, followed closely by her dark-haired older brother. They both stepped into the kitchen, letting the bright sunlight from the screen door fall across their faces.

I froze.

Holy. Shit.

This could *not* be happening.

I knew the boy in front of me. But the last time I'd seen him he'd been shirtless, hungover, and half-asleep. It was the boy who'd thrown the graduation party. The boy I'd run out on after getting drunk enough to go all the way with him.

I had a flash of his lips on my neck, his slurred voice asking, "Is this okay?" My cheeks burned.

"You," he said, his brown eyes wide.

"Do you two know each other?" Dad asked.

"No," I said immediately.

"We went to the same high school," the boy answered.

Sylvia seemed ecstatic about this. "Oh, you went to Fairmont, too?" she asked, moving her hand to my shoulder. She was very touchy. "Greg, you never told me that."

Beside me, Dad looked sheepish. "I thought the school was called Fairview.... Shows how good my memory is."

"Oh, Whitley, if I'd known you two lived *that* close to each other, I would have asked your father to pick you kids up at the same time instead of letting Nathan take a bus last night."

Nathan. So that was his name.

"I can't believe you two went to school together." Sylvia laughed. "What are the odds?"

"Small world," I growled.

"Very," Nathan said. He was smiling now, but I could tell it was forced. At least I wasn't the only one uncomfortable here. Stiffly, he extended his hand to me. "Nice to finally meet you, Whit."

"Whitley," I corrected, reluctantly taking his hand and shaking it for just a second before letting go.

"And this is my daughter," Sylvia said. She gestured to the blond girl — thank God, I didn't know this one — who stepped forward. "Whitley, this is Bailey. She's thirteen, getting ready to start high school in the fall. She's very excited to have a girl around to hang with."

26

"Mom!" Bailey snapped, cheeks red.

"What?" Sylvia asked. "You are, aren't you?"

Bailey turned to me, clearly embarrassed, and said, "Hi, Whitley. It's nice to meet you."

"Yeah...you, too."

"Isn't this great, munchkin?" Dad said, stepping up beside Sylvia and putting his arm around her. "You kids will have a wonderful time together. Won't this be a fun summer?"

Fun? *Fun* was not the word I would have chosen. *Unbearable, awkward, torturous*...Anything but *fun*.

This was a nightmare.

I was supposed to be at the condo, wasting time on the beach, just Dad and me, figuring out college and my life and spending time together. Instead, I was in a new house with new people — including a future stepbrother who'd seen me naked.

"Well." I sighed, facing my father again. "It will definitely be interesting. That's for sure."

4

Sylvia asked Nathan to show me to my new bedroom. Talk about irony.

"This is it," he said, pushing open the second door on the left when we reached the top of the stairs. "Right across the hall from mine."

"Great," I muttered, stepping into the room with my arms folded tightly across my chest. It wasn't small, but it wasn't very big, either. The walls were painted a boring shade of white, and they didn't even have any paintings or pictures hanging on them, which gave the place an eerie psych-ward feel.

My gaze moved to the queen-size bed in the middle of the room. It wasn't the bed I'd slept in at Dad's condo, the bed I'd called mine for six years. This one was larger, with an oak frame and way too many pillows. The comforter was a neutral shade of beige, matching easily with the carpet and the curtains that hung around the only window. It was perfect and clean and pretty, just like everything else in my dad's new life.

And I hated it.

The thing that stung — the thing that was most obvious to me — was that this room was meant to be a guest room. It wasn't mine.

My bedroom at Dad's condo hadn't been fancy or anything. The old bed creaked, and the carpet really needed to be redone. A few photos of Dad and me were the only things that had decorated the walls (aside from one of his crazy bright paintings); I'd never taken the time to put up posters. But the room had been *mine*. No one slept there but me. Even during the school year, I knew Dad hadn't used my room for visitors. He had a spare room for that. My room had belonged to me and only me.

This room didn't. It never would.

"Did you know?" I demanded, turning to face Nathan. The anger over everything I'd learned in the past hour was finally boiling over. "The other night, did you know we were...?"

He sighed and calmly shut the bedroom door. "No. I mean — yes, I knew Greg had a daughter, but I never asked what her name was. I had no idea it was you."

"Right." I walked over to the window and stared down into the backyard, noting the fancy-looking patio strewn with lawn chairs and a table with an umbrella in the middle. I could also see the big-ass inground pool. The water was crystal blue, and a diving board stood at the far end. Just the kind of thing you'd see on TV. "This sucks."

He didn't say anything. He was so calm, taking this so well. I kind of wanted to punch him, to make him yell the way I wanted to yell. Couldn't he see how fucked up this was?

I squeezed my eyes shut and clenched my fingers around the windowsill. My summer wasn't supposed to start like this.

"I won't tell them," he said, breaking the long silence. "You don't have to worry about your dad finding out."

"I don't really give a shit what you tell them." I opened my eyes and turned away from the window, walking over to unzip my duffel bag.

Okay, that wasn't true. I did care. I didn't want Dad to know about the things I'd done. With Nathan or anyone else. No matter how angry I was at him, I still wanted him to see me as his little girl.

But I admit, I would have loved to see Sylvia's face when she found out a member of her perfect little family had thrown a wild party and slept with a girl he barely knew. She'd be scandalized.

"Either way, you don't have to worry about it. Obviously I'd be in trouble, too. So as far as I'm concerned, that party never happened."

"Awesome. Are you done now?" I asked.

Our eyes met then, and he wasn't smiling anymore. Not even that fake cover-up smile. He took a slow, deep breath before saying, "Sorry. I'll let you unpack."

30

"How are you so calm about this?" I cried as he walked toward the door.

Nathan didn't look at me. He kept one hand on the knob, but hesitated before turning it. "We have to spend two and a half months living under the same roof. I think we should both just forget what happened the other night and start from scratch. So, like I said, that party never happened." He opened the door. "Good luck getting settled in. I'll be across the hall if you need anything."

And he walked away.

I closed and locked the door behind him. Forget it ever happened? He made that sound so easy. I knew I'd told him he'd forget about me in no time, but I hadn't expected to be living across the hall. I hated him for making it sound so simple.

With a sigh, I walked back over to my open duffel bag and stared down at my clothes, thrown haphazardly into the bottom. I never folded things. I didn't see the point; I'd just wear them and they'd get all crumpled again anyway. Folding T-shirts was a ridiculous waste of energy.

I grabbed an armful of clothes and went to put them away, but I stopped in the middle of the room. I stared at the double doors of the closet, which I knew must be humongous. It was probably full of linens, I realized. There was probably an old ironing board inside, or maybe a collapsible treadmill. It wasn't *my* closet. It wasn't meant for *my* crap.

So I put the clothes back in my bag. I wasn't about to unpack. Not here. This wasn't home.

I was thinking of digging out the bottle of Margaritaville Gold at the bottom of my duffel. I'd brought it for the nights when Dad and I mixed drinks together. He preferred to use rum, which I wasn't a fan of, so I'd packed my own tequila this summer. It looked like I was going to need it sooner than I thought, though.

I was about to reach into my bag and find it when someone knocked on the door.

"What?"

"Um . . . Can I come in?"

I frowned and walked across the room. After flipping the lock, I pulled the door open a crack and looked out into the hall. Bailey was standing there, running her fingers through her hair. Now that I got a decent look at her, I realized just how small this girl was. She hadn't even hit five feet yet, and she looked like she might weigh ninety pounds. If Sylvia hadn't mentioned that she was about to start high school, I would have guessed the kid was ten years old.

"Is it okay if I, um, come in?"

"Uh, sure," I said, pulling the door open and stepping aside.

"Thanks." She walked into the room, barely looking around as she moved to plop down on the bed. She glanced at my duffel bag. "You unpacking?"

"No," I said. Before she could ask why, I added, "Do you need something?"

"Oh. No, not really," she answered, shaking her head. "Sorry. I can leave if I'm bothering you. I just thought I'd help you unpack or something."

"Oh."

"Are you okay?" she asked. "I mean, you seem...like, really surprised by all this."

"That's because I am," I said, pushing the door closed again.

"Really? Your dad didn't tell you about us?"

"No."

"How come?"

"You'd have to ask him that."

"Wow...I'm sorry. That kind of sucks." She paused for a moment, then added, "I hope you'll still have fun here, though. I've been looking forward to meeting you. We can, like, hang out. I've never had a sister before."

This will not make us sisters, I thought. I wanted to scream it at her. It took everything I had to hold it back.

"Don't get me wrong," she was saying, unaware of my fuming. "Nathan's okay. We don't fight that much. Not like my friends do with their brothers. He drives me places and takes me to movies. He's all right, but I've always wanted a sister.... You probably think that's stupid, don't you?"

"Pretty much." She looked suddenly hurt when I said this, and I felt kind of guilty, so I added, "I mean, I sort of get it. I have a big brother, too, but he moved out years ago, so I haven't really been much of a sister in a while. I probably suck at it."

"I'm sure you don't," she said. "I love your clothes. Those jeans are awesome. We could, like, hang out and go shopping if you want. I need some new clothes for high school, and, well, Mom said she'd take me, but…she has really bad taste. She always puts me in this old-woman-looking stuff. Stuff no one my age wears. I'd rather dress the way you do."

I looked down at my green cotton tank top and low-slung Tommy Hilfiger jeans. "Thanks." The girl deserved some credit. At least she knew good fashion when she saw it. If there was one thing I cared about, it was my wardrobe, and I had certainly mastered the "I don't give a shit" look. Believe it or not, it took a lot of talent to pull off that style without looking sloppy.

"We should definitely go shopping," she said again.

"Um…maybe."

"Awesome," she said. "My birthday is in August. I'll have money after that. We could go to the mall in the next county over before you leave for college. That would be fun."

"Maybe," I repeated. I wasn't committing myself to anything. But it was impossible to flat out reject this girl. I wasn't a pushover or anything. Far from it. She just had those big puppy eyes that made you feel guilty, you know?

That's why, when she asked, "Do you want me to go? So you can unpack and get settled in?" I shook my head and let her stay.

"So do you, like, have a boyfriend?" she asked, pulling her legs into a crisscross position on the bed. "Is he going to miss you while you're here?"

"I don't have one," I told her. "And I don't want one, either."

"Why not?" she asked.

"Boys are a pain in the ass."

Bailey laughed, like she thought I was kidding. "I'm allowed to date once I start high school. I'm going to try out for the cheerleading squad this summer. Boys like cheerleaders, right?"

"I guess," I said, walking over to stare out the window. "I wouldn't really know. I didn't hang out with the cheerleaders much. We weren't in the same crowd."

"So what crowd *were* you in?"

I looked over at her, thinking of how to answer.

I remembered being thirteen and thinking that high school would be some great new adventure. I'd even dreamed of being a cheerleader, too. At the time, though, I'd been in the middle of an awkward growth spurt. I was all knees and elbows, and I could barely walk without tripping, let alone do a decent cartwheel.

By the time tryouts rolled around the next year, though, my ambitions had changed. I'd started partying and drinking and getting a reputation for being easy, which was funny, I guess, since I wasn't even having sex when the rumors first started. The prissy little cheerleaders thought I was a wild-child slut, and I thought they were stupid bitches. So it just hadn't worked out.

It was weird to think I'd been so much like Bailey once.

I cleared my throat, suddenly aware that she was still waiting on my answer. "Well, I was in the . . . the . . ."

"Bailey!" Sylvia's voice called from downstairs. "Honey, come help me set the table for supper."

"Coming!" Bailey yelled. She hopped off the bed and walked over to the door, looking back at me with that same happy smile. "We'll hang out again later, okay?"

"Sure," I mumbled.

"We eat dinner at six," she added. "I'll see you downstairs in a little while, Whitley."

Then she was gone.

And I was finally alone.

"You've got to be kidding me. Getting married?"

"Yeah. This fall."

"Wow." Mom was quiet for a moment before asking, "So...what's she like?"

I scowled at the phone in my hand, wishing she could see the annoyance on my face. "I don't know, Mom. She's a lawyer, has two kids, lives like freaking Martha Stewart. Does it matter?"

"Is she pretty?"

"Yes. Gorgeous. Is that what you're hoping to hear?"

I wanted to throw my phone across the room, to scream. Even this was about her. About Dad moving on without her. About how she compared to Sylvia. She didn't even seem to think about me.

"Sorry, sorry," Mom said with a sniffle. Was she crying?

A weight pressed into my chest, and I wished I hadn't snapped at her.

I still remembered the days when she'd make me call in and lie to her boss, tell him that she was sick and couldn't come in. The days when I ate only cereal because she wouldn't even get up to cook. She hadn't done that in years, not to that extent, at least, but this could be the thing to send her over the edge again.

"Mom, I'm just...I'm really upset right now. This is all piling up on me at once, you know?"

"Oh, I understand. God, this is so *your father*. I can't believe he didn't warn you. He is so selfish."

I gritted my teeth. Now she was going too far in the other direction. Did she really think this was helping me? I didn't even know why I called her. I guess...I just wanted to talk to *someone*. I wanted someone to listen to me complain and to sympathize with me for a few minutes. I wanted someone to understand how lost I felt.

I had tried to call Trace first, but all I got was his voice mail. And this wasn't exactly something you left on the machine: *Hey, did you know Dad is engaged to Carol Brady? No? Well he is and I'm pissed. Please make me feel better.*

Mom was my only other option. I didn't have friends I could turn to. I didn't have anyone. But calling her had clearly been a mistake.

"I'm going to call him," Mom declared, her sniffles gone, voice turned furious. "I'm going to tell him exactly what I think of this whole monstrosity. I'm —"

"No, Mom," I said. "Just…just leave it alone. It's my fault.…Neither of us is a phone person — I should have made the effort to call him or something."

"Don't make excuses for him, Whitley. He's so —"

"Munchkin! Nate! Come on down, kids. Dinner's ready!"

"Mom, I have to go. I'll call you later."

I snapped the phone shut before she had time to respond.

With a groan, I rolled off the bed and put my cell on the nightstand. As glad as I was to end that conversation, I still kind of wanted to come up with some sort of excuse — *Daddy, I have a headache; I feel sick to my stomach* — to get out of eating dinner with June Cleaver and her perfect children.

Unfortunately for me, I was starving.

Nathan walked out of his room just as I stepped out of mine. We both just kind of looked at each other for a weird second, then turned and headed toward the stairs. "So…munchkin, huh?" he said. "Aren't you a little tall to be a munchkin?"

"I had a growth spurt when I was thirteen," I replied without thinking. "Dad just hasn't found a more fitting nickname yet."

"Ah." He nodded. "Well, my granddad still calls Mom his Sylvie Bear, so I guess it's a universal thing."

I rolled my eyes and moved ahead of him, hurrying down the last few steps. I didn't need his forced conversation. If he wanted to forget what happened the other night, we could forget in silence.

"Hey, Whitley," Sylvia said when I walked into the dining room. "I hope you're making yourself comfortable."

"Sure," I muttered. *Of course I'm not comfortable, you Stepford Wife. This is, like, my worst nightmare.*

"Good," she said. "I really want you to enjoy this summer with us."

"Whatever." I glanced around the large oak-paneled room. Talk about fancy. Expensive-looking paintings hung from nails or rested against the wall, waiting to be put in their proper place. Every piece of furniture — all made of sleek, polished wood — looked brand-new. Of course, it probably was new. Clearly, Sylvia was one of the rich kinds of lawyers.

"Don't worry, babe," Dad said, grinning at Sylvia from his seat. "She'll have a great time."

I started to pull out a chair, but Sylvia stopped me. "Oh, honey, Bailey wants you to sit next to her."

"Mom!" Bailey shrieked from the other end of the dining table.

"Well, you do want her sitting by you. You just said so a minute ago," Sylvia said, sounding a little defensive. "Can I say anything that won't embarrass you today?"

"Only if you want to," Bailey insisted, turning to look at me and ignoring her mother's question. "It's cool if you don't. No big. I just thought —"

Without saying anything, I walked around the table and pulled out the chair between my dad and Bailey. Sitting by her would be better than being next to Nathan, who'd just plopped down in the chair beside his mother.

I glanced over at Sylvia and Nathan, expecting to overhear some *Leave It to Beaver*–esque dinner conversation. But

40

their end of the table was quiet. Nathan was smiling, but Sylvia examined Nathan closely, intently. Maybe her supermom sense was tingling. I wondered just how much she'd freak if she knew about Nathan and me and the party.

"Hey, Nate, do you mind passing the mashed potatoes this way?"

Nathan spooned out an overlarge helping of mashed potatoes before passing the bowl to Dad. "Here you go, Greg. They're awesome."

"Anything your mother cooks is awesome," Dad replied.

Gag me.

"Oh, stop." Sylvia laughed, and the tension I thought I'd seen in her face moments before vanished. Maybe it was just wishful thinking. I just wanted to see a problem with this arrangement. A gap. An imperfection. "You two are too sweet."

"Nate's the sweet one," Dad said. "I just agree with him and reap the benefits. It's a wonderful job."

Nate, I thought. They were buddies. Dad already fit in here, with this family. He was one of them.

And I wasn't.

Looking around the table, I realized just how out of place I was. The Caulfields and Dad were smiling. They were all dressed in bright, happy, summery colors. And me? I'd been fixed with a permanent scowl. I liked cold colors — dark greens and blues. And, to be honest, I didn't think I'd really been *happy* in a long time.

"So, munchkin," Dad said, suddenly noticing me. This

wasn't really Dad, though. He sounded more mature and fatherly than the real Greg Johnson ever did. It was like his newscaster alter ego was speaking to me. A show just for the Caulfields.

My real dad was laid back. Outside of work, he was casual and uncensored and funny. He swore and sang classic rock songs he barely knew the lyrics to — especially after he'd knocked back a few shots on the beach. I wanted to know where that man was. I wanted to know what Sylvia had done to change him.

She'd taken him away from me.

"What do you think of the house?" he asked in the TV-Dad voice. "Is your room okay?"

"Fine," I lied, taking the bowl of green beans from Bailey.

That was something else I didn't get. This family-dinner thing. Dad ate his microwavable meals in front of the TV, usually watching ESPN Classic. At the condo, on the nights when he grilled, we'd eat outside while the radio blasted Jimmy Buffett and he and his girlfriend of the moment drank margaritas. Dinner meant scratching itchy summer mosquito bites and hiding the scraps of burned hamburger in my napkin to avoid hurting Dad's feelings.

"You'll love Hamilton," Sylvia said as she buttered a roll.

I glared at her. This was all her fault. Sure, Dad should have told me about this, but if she hadn't just barged into his life, putting on her flashy Martha Stewart–inspired song and dance, there wouldn't have been anything to tell. I hated her.

"Of course she will," Dad said. "It's a great place for teenagers, too, munchkin. Nathan, have you told Whitley about the Nest?"

"I hadn't gotten around to it yet."

"When can we go?" Bailey asked. "Can we go tomorrow night? Will you come with us, Whitley?"

"Go where?" Her enthusiasm made me uneasy.

"The Nest," Sylvia answered, sounding stiff but still wearing that annoying smile. "It's a little dance club for teenagers."

"They have bands and music and food," Dad explained. "It's a nice, safe, wholesome place for local teenagers to spend time. Sherri, Sylvia's sister, says it's packed with high school students every weekend. And during the summer, it's open all week long. I told Nate he should take you and Bailey-Boop."

I cringed. *Bailey-Boop?* The nickname made me want to barf almost as much as Dad's description of the Nest. A "wholesome" place to hang out? Seriously? Already I knew that this place would not be my scene. If there wasn't alcohol to distract me from all this shit, I wasn't interested.

"So can we go tomorrow night?" Bailey asked Nathan across the table. "Please?"

"That's up to Whit," he said.

"Whitley," I growled.

I hated — and I mean *hated* — being called "Whit." For Christ's sake, my parents named me Whitley for a reason. If they'd wanted me to be called Whit, that's what they would have written on my birth certificate.

"So, you up for it tomorrow night?" Nathan asked, like he hadn't heard me.

"I don't know, Nathan." Sylvia was watching him. "I'm not sure if it's a good idea. Maybe you should stay in."

"I'd love to go." I looked right at Nathan. "It sounds great."

"Oh, honey. Let them have some fun," Dad said. "It's summertime. They're kids. A night out won't hurt."

Sylvia looked distinctly unhappy. Good. I might have to spend tomorrow night at a lame club with her spawn, but if that meant pissing her off, it was so worth it.

"Fine," she relented. "Just behave yourselves."

"You three will have a good time," Dad said, handing me the plate of rolls. "This will be a chance for you to bond. Become friends."

"Awesome." Bailey grinned at me. "I'll have to figure out what I'll wear."

Then Dad was talking about some special report he was airing the next morning and Sylvia returned to her smiling, bubbly ways. The dent I'd tried to make in her perfect little meal didn't seem to matter. Of course not.

When everyone was done, Nathan offered to help Sylvia clean up. As I walked out of the dining room, I heard him say quietly, "Mom, it'll be fine."

I thought about lingering, eavesdropping to see what he meant, but Sylvia caught me in the doorway and gave me that smile again. "Do you want Bailey to help you set up your room?" she asked.

I shook my head and walked away.

When I got upstairs, I locked the door and dug out my

bottle of cheap tequila. If there was one thing that would cheer me up, it was booze.

Later, as I lay stretched out on the bed, I glanced at the bottle on the nightstand. Sylvia would freak if she knew I'd brought alcohol into her house. The thought made me laugh. They were so perfect, so proper and clean. Dad and Sylvia and Nathan and Bailey — they were all downstairs, probably watching a fun family movie and playing Monopoly. And I was upstairs, alone, drunk on Margaritaville Gold.

I didn't fit in with them at all.

It was so funny, so funny I couldn't remember why I'd been angry before.

I laughed until it hurt, until the room spun, until I closed my eyes and fell asleep.

6

The next day I woke to the sound of Bobby Brown singing "My Prerogative." I sighed and rolled over, groping blindly for my phone on the nightstand and knocking over the bottle of tequila by accident.

"Shit," I muttered. Thank God the bottle was closed, or that would have been a bitch to explain.

A second later, I found my cell and flipped it open. "Hello?"

"Hey, sis. Saw you called. Sorry I couldn't talk last night. We had to take Marie to the doctor."

"Huh? Oh, Marie... Is she okay?"

"Fine. Emily just got freaked out about a little fever. But you sound awful. You hungover?"

"A little."

"God, Whitley."

"Did you know Dad is getting married?" I asked.

"What? No."

"Yep. Her name is Sylvia. She's a widow with two kids. She and Dad met last September."

"Well," he said. "I guess that's nice. If they wait a few months to get married, maybe I can fly out for the wedding with Emily and Marie."

"Is that all you have to say?" I asked.

"What else do you expect me to say?"

I sighed. "I don't know. I hate it, Trace. I don't like how different he is with them. He's not the same Dad we grew up with."

"That might not be a bad thing," Trace grumbled.

"What's that supposed to mean?"

"Whitley, you were pretty young during those last few years Mom and Dad were together. There was a lot you didn't —" I could hear Marie starting to scream in the background. "*Shit*, Emily's at the drugstore and I've got Marie — she just woke up." I could hear him shift the phone away from his mouth. "Shh, shh, it's okay." I'd been through this before, and I knew the conversation was as good as over. Sure enough, he came back a second later. "I've got to go. I'll talk to you tomorrow, Whitley. Good luck with Dad. Love you. Bye."

Click.

"Hurry up, Whit! We're waiting on you."

"Then get the hell out of here and leave me alone," I

growled to myself as I slipped a navy blue tank over my head and turned to examine myself in the bathroom mirror. I wondered if Sylvia would be offended by the way my black bra straps showed. I really hoped so.

I applied a little bit of black eyeliner and a dab of lip gloss.

Honestly, I didn't expect to have any fun at this "wholesome" club, but I did hope to meet someone who could tell me where the real party was. Towns this small still had parties, right? I figured if I was going to be stuck here all summer, I needed to find out where to have a decent time. That bottle of Margaritaville Gold wasn't going to last me long.

I'd never had to go looking for a good time during the summer before. Hanging out with Dad, watching movies and talking over dinner and listening to music at the condo... That had been enough.

This summer was different, though. Dad was different. He didn't care about me this year. And I wasn't going to let myself go insane in this house for three months.

"Whit!" Nathan yelled again.

"Give me a second! *Shit.*"

I really did need to hurry up, though. It was already seven, and Bailey had been completely made up, wearing her pink cocktail dress and strappy white sandals, since five.

The sad part was that I knew she'd leave the Nest disappointed. Sure, Bailey was all excited to go to this little teen club, but it wasn't as if she'd make friends. She probably wouldn't even talk to anyone. She'd cling to Nathan or me the whole night and come home feeling like crap. That's how it always went. I know it sounds cynical or bitchy to say, but it's true.

I put on my flip-flops and started walking downstairs. They were waiting by the door, Bailey fidgeting with her dress. She looked like she was ready for a Homecoming dance, not a nightclub. On the other hand, Nathan was totally casual. Ripped blue jeans, faded band T-shirt, sloppy hair. He looked like a mess next to his sister.

I was surprised Perfect Sylvia let one of her Perfect Offspring dress with such imperfection.

"Ready?" Nathan asked, pulling car keys from his pocket.

"You kids have fun," Dad said from the sofa, turning a page in the novel he was reading. "Get to know each other. You're family now."

Yeah, I thought. *Family who've banged each other.*

"Be careful," Sylvia said. She was standing in the doorway between the living room and kitchen, her arms crossed over her chest. She looked a little on edge. One minute this chick was bubbly as could be, and the next she looked all uptight and anxious. "I'll expect you home by ten thirty."

"No problem," Nathan said, giving the adults a casual wave before turning to his sister and me. "Let's go, shall we?"

Bailey was already out the door, running down the steps, golden hair streaming behind her. She stopped abruptly in the middle of the sidewalk, glancing over her shoulder at us. Her face turned a little pink, as if she were embarrassed by her own excitement.

Nathan looked at me and shrugged. "Ladies first," he said, holding the front door open.

I moved past him and headed for the car. Bailey smiled at me as she climbed into the backseat.

"I've never been to a club before," she said once I'd gotten comfortable in the passenger's seat. "I mean, like, I've been to my friends' parties and stuff — obviously. But they were kind of boring. A club will be cooler, right?"

"Um...sure."

Nathan climbed into the car and immediately turned on the air conditioner. The sun was still out, and despite it being mid-evening, the air was scorching hot and so humid I thought I'd drown. "Buckle up," he said to me, hitting the button for the radio.

He waited until my seat belt had clicked before he even pulled out of the driveway. As if traveling those three extra feet without restraints might actually kill me or something. I didn't expect someone who had one-night stands with strangers or threw crazy parties to have such a stick up his ass.

I didn't say anything on the way to the Nest. Bailey jabbered away at us from the backseat, speculating on the kind of music they'd play, what the other girls there might be wearing, how crowded the place might be. After a while, Nathan cranked up the radio as a subtle hint that she should quiet down. A hint that she, eventually, took.

The silence didn't last long, though. A minute later Nathan was singing along with the radio, tapping his fingers against the wheel to keep the beat. I couldn't help watching, a moment from the party sliding into my memory. We'd been kissing in the armchair, amid the chaos of dancing and drinking, when Van Morrison's "Brown Eyed Girl" started playing through the speakers.

Nathan had pulled back a little, giving me a second to come up for air. He grinned at me and started singing along with the song — off-key, but he was pretty drunk by then, so I guess that was to be expected. I reached up and clapped a hand over his mouth, laughing. "Stop. You can't sing at all."

Clumsily, he took hold of my wrist and eased it away from his lips. "I love this song, even if it is really old," he slurred.

"Me, too."

"Good, then it can be our song. You're my brown-eyed girl."

"But my eyes are blue," I told him.

"I know. But there aren't songs about blue eyes."

I started laughing harder and almost fell off Nathan's lap. "Yes there are. 'Blue Eyes Crying in the Rain,' 'Behind Blue Eyes,' 'The Bluest Eyes in Texas,' and then there's just 'Blue Eyes' by Elton John."

"Yeah?" he said. "Well, those suck."

"You suck."

And then we were kissing again. It couldn't have been long after that that we migrated to the bedroom.

Three days later, sitting in the car beside him, part of me wondered if it had really happened. He'd said that as far as he was concerned that night had never occurred, but could

51

he really forget so easily? Probably not, but he acted like he could. He acted way better than I did.

He parked the car in front of the small brick building and cut the engine. "Behold," he said. "The Nest."

Honestly, the place looked kind of run-down, but the parking lot was packed with cars. Either it was actually a cool place (I kind of doubted it) or there was nothing better to do in this town.

When Nathan pushed open the front door for Bailey and me, I knew it was definitely the second theory.

First of all, the band blew. Though I admit I was impressed to see a band at all. The lead singer had zero talent, and the drummer had no rhythm whatsoever. It was just sickening, really. I knew people who had more musical ability than these guys when they were plastered. Myself included. And the sad excuse for a dance floor was half the size of the guest room at Dad's new place. The walls were lined with booths, all packed with teenagers sipping on sodas or bobbing their heads to the music.

"Wow," I heard Bailey murmur, and I could tell she was overwhelmed — whether by how pathetic the place was or by the number of people, I wasn't sure.

"I'm thirsty," Nathan said. "Let's get drinks. What do you want, Whit?"

"Nothing." I was already walking away from them. "I'll get it myself."

I'd decided early on that if I was going to track down some fun — i.e., boys and booze — I needed to ditch Nathan and Bailey. I couldn't afford to have them cockblocking me tonight.

After scanning the room once, I came to the conclusion that the selection of guys here sucked. I mean, they were average, I guess, but none of them were hot. Because of this, I was feeling a little disappointed when I made my second turn around the dance floor.

Then I saw the sexy tanned boy sitting at the bar.

He wasn't tall, but he had the dark and the handsome parts down. His hair was a sleek, shiny black, and his eyes were huge emerald spotlights in the dim lighting of the club. Smoldering hot, and well dressed, too. He had on a nice, neat button-up shirt and black jeans.

Target acquired.

I approached the bar, tossing back my long hair and giving him my best seductive smile. I eased up right next to him. "Hey," I said, winking. "What's up?"

He grinned. Rows of straight, glittering white teeth. "Do I know you?"

"Nope, but you want to." I slid onto the barstool next to his.

"What's your name?" he asked.

"Yours first."

"Harrison Carlyle," he said, sounding a little amused. *"Now* do I get your name?"

"Whitley Johnson."

Harrison's eyes widened and he sat up a little straighter as he looked me over. My moves must have been working — he was already interested. *Awesome,* I thought. Even if he didn't know where I could find a party, I wouldn't mind fooling around with him. That was one thing I loved about boys — if I wanted a quick, meaningless hookup just for fun, they were never very hard to convince.

I was wondering how much chitchat we'd have to make before I could get Harrison to take me somewhere private... and then he started talking.

"Oh my God!" he said excitedly. "Are you — You have to be! You're totally related to Greg Johnson, aren't you? The news guy. Are you his daughter? You are, right?"

"Um...yeah. He's my dad."

"That is *so* cool," he cried. "I still can't believe he moved here. No one famous lives in this place. I know he's not a movie star or anything, but still. He's on TV, which is a big deal around here. We love him."

"Thanks." Great. I was the one with boobs, but the boy had a thing for my dad. What the hell? Okay. It was time for a subject change.

"So," I said, crossing my legs. I was wearing a short white skirt, showing off plenty of skin. Too bad it wasn't quite tanned yet. "What all is there to do around here?"

"Absolutely nothing," he answered, shrugging his broad shoulders. "We live in the lamest town ever. You just kind of get used to it."

"Well..." I swiveled in my seat a little, turning so I could press my leg right up against his. My signature move. Worked every time. "We could make it exciting, if you want. I'm a pretty exciting girl."

Then he started laughing at me.

Not the reaction I was going for.

"Oh, honey." He reached out suddenly and took my hand in both of his. "You're cute. You really, really are, but I'm not interested."

"Why not?" I asked point-blank. No use wondering about it for weeks or letting my self-image plummet because of this loser. Might as well cut to the chase.

Harrison sighed and took one of his hands away from mine. "See that guy over there, with the blond?" he asked, pointing.

My eyes followed in the direction he indicated. Across the room, sitting at a booth by themselves, were Nathan and Bailey. Even from here, I could tell Bailey looked disappointed. Nathan was chatting with her, moving his arms in big, over-the-top gestures. He must have been trying to cheer her up.

"I see him," I said, nodding. "That's my...future stepbrother." I choked on the last two words.

"For real?" Harrison asked.

"Yeah."

"That sucks for you. I could just eat him up."

I gawked at him. "What?"

"That's why I'm not interested," he explained calmly, like I was an irrational five-year-old. "Your stepbrother over there, he's more my type...if you know what I mean."

And, of course, I knew what he meant.

It figured. The one boy in this place I was interested in

was not interested in me. After all the shit I'd dealt with over the last two days, getting shot down was just the icing on the cake. But I tried to soothe my ego with the fact that it wasn't *me* he wasn't interested in, it was all girls. Still, not what I needed tonight.

"Shit," I muttered, slumping back against the bar with my arms folded over my chest.

"I'm sorry," he said, squeezing my shoulder. "It's nothing personal. You're a hottie, but boobs just aren't my thing."

"Whatever."

He smiled. "I still can't believe you're Greg Johnson's daughter. That's so awesome."

"It isn't that glamorous.... Actually, it sucks ass at the moment."

"How is that possible?" Harrison asked. "He is so *hot*."

"My dad? Christ, that's gross."

"He is."

"Ew."

He reached forward and put a hand on my knee. It was the least sexy knee-rub in the history of knee-rubs. "You get your looks from him, if it helps."

"Thanks. But that is still gross."

He laughed and grabbed his glass of soda. "What a pout you've got on you," he said, lifting the drink to his lips.

What a jerk. My misery was *not* funny. Or cute.

"Here," he said, putting his glass back down on the rickety bar. "Let me buy you a drink. What do you want?"

No matter how frustrated I felt, a free drink just wasn't something I could turn down.

"Something strong," I groaned.

"Coca-Cola strong enough?"

"Hardly."

He shook his head and looked down the bar. "Joe!" he called. "Hey, honey, can you get the pretty girl a Coke?"

"Only if you stop calling me *honey*," the bartender, a bearded man in his thirties, replied. "We've had this discussion before, Harrison."

"Aw, Joe. It's so cute that you think I listen."

The bartender poured some Coke into a glass and slid it toward me. Harrison winked and handed the cash to Joe, who rolled his eyes before walking back to the other end of the bar, where more customers waited.

"He hates it when I flirt with him," Harrison whispered to me. "Which just makes it funnier."

I laughed and reached for my Coke. "Thanks," I said, taking a big gulp. I tried to pretend it was tequila — or even just beer — but my body knew better. Goddamn it, I couldn't even trick myself out of sobriety. Like those cases you hear about sometimes, when people have convinced themselves they were drunk through the power of persuasion. I wanted to persuade myself that I was wasted.

Apparently, I'm not very gullible.

I took another drink, wishing I'd thought to smuggle my bottle of cheap tequila in with me.

"So, how long are you in Hamilton for?"

"Just the summer," I said. "Then it's off to University of Kentucky."

"Nice. What major?"

"No fucking idea." I sighed. "Kind of hoping Dad will help me figure it out this summer. He went to UK, too. What about you?"

"I graduated a year ago, but I took a year off to figure out all the 'rest of my life' stuff, so I know how you feel. But I'm off to UCLA this fall. I'm majoring in fashion design. Maybe not the smartest choice, but it's what I love."

"California," I mused. "I bet you'll be happy to get out of this shithole."

He shrugged. "I guess. You know, the place is lame, but it's home. And it's not that bad if you know where to go. You just have to have friends."

"Then I'm screwed."

He chuckled. "Tell you what. I'll be your friend, okay?"

"I don't really do friends," I told him.

"Good," he said. "I don't want you to 'do' me. We've established the flaws in that plan already. But we can hang out. Oh, or shop. Your outfit is super cute.... Though I'm not a fan of the flip-flops. They look cheap."

"Thanks, Tim Gunn. Anything else you'd like to critique?"

"I'm just being honest. You're a fashion slut."

"Excuse me?"

"You have good taste, but you're stepping into too many

58

styles," he said. "Those flip-flops might be all the rage this season, but they don't fit you. The rest of your look doesn't scream 'beach babe.' Nope. You need to stick with one style. For you, I'd say that style is sexy-casual. Oh, some nice wedge sandals would be perfect for you."

"You don't even know me," I reminded him. "What gives you the right to analyze my *style*?"

"You're right," he agreed. "I don't know you, but I do know fashion. I'm gay, remember? Do you really want to argue wardrobe choices with me?"

"Just because you're gay doesn't mean you get to bandy about that horrible stereotype. I've partied with tons of gay guys who sucked with clothes," I pointed out.

Harrison shrugged. "They weren't me."

Reluctantly, I looked down at my flip-flops. I hated to admit it, but he was right. Now that I thought about it, they really didn't go with the rest of the outfit. They looked kind of tacky with the little plastic flowers along the straps. It just didn't work for me. Less sexy, more little-girl cutesy.

"So, are you going to argue?" he asked again, clearly watching as I examined the footwear faux pas.

"No," I mumbled. "I'm not going to argue with you."

"Good call."

It didn't seem like any time had passed when I saw Nathan approaching us, jingling car keys in his right hand. Somehow, Harrison had managed to pull me into a conversation about the best and worst name-brand fashion designers, so I didn't even see him coming until Harrison's emerald eyes lit up like lightbulbs and a Cheshire Cat smirk began to spread across his face.

"Hey," Nathan said, stopping next to my stool. "Ready to get out of here?"

"This soon?"

Nathan looked over at Harrison, then turned back to me. "Sorry," he said. "But Bailey's ready to go. She says she doesn't feel well."

Classic cop-out, I thought. *Is that the best excuse the kid could come up with?*

"Hello there." Harrison winked at me as he extended his hand toward Nathan. "I'm Harrison Carlyle. You must be Whitley's stepbrother."

"Not yet," Nathan said. "Our parents don't get married until sometime in September. I'm Nathan, by the way. I'm sure Whit told you that."

"*Whit-ley*," I snarled. "With two syllables."

"She is so lucky to see your handsome face every morning," Harrison told Nathan. "Many people would kill to be in her position."

"Ha. I doubt that, but thanks." Nathan laughed. "I'll meet you in the car, Whit. Bailey's already outside."

"Fine."

Nathan nodded to Harrison once before turning and walking out the front door of the club.

Harrison practically swooned. "Now *that* is beauty. I

mean, that body? Tall and lean...You can't tell me there aren't a few dirty things you'd like to do to him."

"Not really," I said, mentally adding, *I've already done them.* Slowly, I stood up. "I should go."

"Okay," he said. "But I really liked talking to you. We should do this again."

"Yeah, we'll see."

The truth was, as cool as Harrison had seemed, what I'd told him was true. I didn't really do the whole "friends" thing. Not since middle school, anyway. In my experience, friends turned on you, abandoned you, lied about you. The best kind of "friends" were the ones you played beer pong with at a party and never saw again. I just wasn't looking to make friends.

I was already moving away when he caught my elbow.

"Actually," he said, spinning me to face him again. The guy was pretty strong, I'll give him that. "My best friend is having a party at his house. You should come."

I wasn't looking for friends, but I *was* looking for a party.

"Will it be as lame as this place?" I asked, gesturing to the stage, where the shitty band attempted to fix their malfunctioning sound equipment.

"Oh, God, no," Harrison assured me. "This party will be killer. He lives in a freaking mansion. You should come and hang out. I'll introduce you to everyone. It'll be fun."

"Will there be drinks?"

"Yes."

"Besides Coke. I mean, like, beer or —"

"*Yes*," Harrison insisted. "There will be."

"Then I'll be there."

"Fabulous. Don't wear those flip-flops, for God's sake."

"I won't," I told him, handing over my cell so he could program his number into my phone book. I'd call and get the address later. "I promise."

"Great."

He handed back my phone and I started to walk away again, but Harrison yelled after me, managing to raise his voice over the loud feedback from the ancient speakers. I turned to look at him one more time.

"It's this Saturday night," he said. "Do you think you could get Nathan to come?" There was that hope again. That same bright sparkle I saw in Bailey's eyes. But this one... this one I had to crush. For Harrison's own good.

"He's straight," I said.

"How straight?"

"He sleeps with girls, so I'd say pretty straight."

Harrison's face fell, but only for a second. "Oh, well. He should still come. The party will be a blast. I'll see you there."

I nodded and, finally, managed to walk all the way out the door.

7

It was _way_ too early the next morning when Sylvia knocked on the door of the guest room. Like, eight-o-freaking-clock. I rolled out of bed, feeling distinctly murderous, and stumbled across the room.

"Yeah?" I said, pulling the door open a crack.

"Do you want breakfast?" she asked, showing all of her perfect teeth when she smiled. I saw a sudden flash of what she might look like if I knocked out a few of them.

She was already dressed in a navy suit and those superhigh heels. For a second I was confused about why. Then I remembered she must have work, which meant it was Monday. The summer always had me screwed up like that.

"I'm good," I replied, already starting to close the door.

She stuck out the toe of her shoe, forcing me to keep it open. "Do you have plans for this morning?" she asked.

"Um, yeah. Sleep."

She laughed.

That hadn't been a joke.

"Well, there is some money on the counter in case you decide you want to go out," she said. "There's not much to do in Hamilton, I know, but there's a mall and a movie theater in the next county — about twenty minutes from here. I'm sure you or Nathan could look up directions on the computer. And there's plenty of food in the fridge when you get hungry. Your dad will be home around noon, but you can call my cell if you need anything. The number is on the counter."

"I'm eighteen," I told her. "I know how to take care of myself."

She raised an eyebrow at me. "I know you do. I'm just... trying to be helpful."

"Well, thanks, but I'll be fine."

"All right," Sylvia said, eyeing me for a second more. Slowly, she slid her foot out of the door opening. "Then I guess I'm off to work. It's my first day at the new firm, so wish me luck. Bailey and Nathan are downstairs watching TV."

They were seriously awake at this hour? *Dear God, I must be living with aliens.*

"I'll see you tonight," she added, starting down the hallway. "Have a fun day."

"Whatever."

A second later, her heels were clacking down the stairs as she sang an old Donna Summer song under her breath. Now I knew where Nathan got it.

I closed the door and crawled back into the comfy guest bed, burying my face in the pillow and pulling the blankets up to my neck. My eyes squeezed shut as I willed sleep to wash back over me. It wasn't noon yet. I should still be dreaming. Dreaming of things so much better than this summer.

But I was wide awake now, and sleep just wouldn't come.

After twenty minutes, I gave up. I climbed out of bed and walked over to my duffel bag, searching through the mess inside for clothes to wear. Within seconds, though, I came across my bathing suit, tossed among the shorts and T-shirts and rolled-up socks, and I decided exactly what I'd be doing that day.

I slipped off my pajamas and pulled on the hot pink string bikini I'd packed. The thing only covered what was required by law. Maybe there would be some cute boy living next door who'd see me through the fence. Or perhaps Sylvia had enough money to hire a sexy pool boy I could flirt with. After striking out with Harrison, I needed a little bit of ego stroking.

I grabbed my iPod and walked downstairs, not bothering to put on a T-shirt or anything as a cover-up. No point getting something else dirty, after all.

Nathan was making a bowl of cereal at the counter when I walked into the kitchen. He was wearing a pair of black athletic shorts with a rusty-orange-colored T-shirt (how did Harrison like him when he was so poorly dressed?), and he had to push his messy hair out of his eyes. I didn't miss the way those eyes popped when he looked up and saw me. The way his cheeks flushed and his mouth parted a little was all the ego stroking I needed. Apparently he didn't have to be drunk to find me attractive. Good to know.

"Um...hey." He cleared his throat twice. "You...You going swimming?"

"No, just lying out," I said, grabbing a Diet Coke from the fridge.

"Oh. Cool." He turned away, focusing on his hands a little harder than was required to pour milk into a bowl of cereal.

It was interesting seeing calm, collected Nathan looking a little shaken. While I'd been biting my tongue to keep from screaming at dinner every night and downing tequila alone in my bedroom to keep my mind off the awkwardness and frustration, Nathan had seemed completely unaffected. Call me cruel, but I wanted to see him squirm a little.

"Hey, Nathan?" He looked up from his cereal bowl, and I smiled as innocently as I could. "Do you know if anyone would mind me sunbathing topless? Would the neighbors see?"

And here I thought his blush couldn't get any deeper.

"Because," I continued, holding the can of Diet Coke in one hand and tugging lightly at the cord that held my iPod around my neck with the other, "it's just that the tan looks so much...smoother."

Nathan took a deep breath in through his nose and let it out slowly before answering. "There's a chance the people next door might get offended."

"Oh." I sighed. I could see Nathan's eyes following the progress of my hand as I tucked my earbuds into my ears, letting my fingers slide across my neck just a little. "Fine. I guess I'll just get tan lines. Thanks anyway, Nathan."

"Yeah...no problem."

With a smirk, I turned and walked out the sliding glass door.

As far as I could tell, there was no cute pool boy, which was kind of a bummer, but whatever. The look on Nathan's face would have to last me for a while. I slid into a lounge chair, kicking up my bare feet and scrolling through my iPod. I was in the mood for some Madonna. Not her new stuff, but old-school Madonna. Back before the Kabbalah and the MTV make-out with Britney Spears. So I skimmed through my playlist until I found "Like a Prayer," then closed my eyes, letting the sound and sun wash over me.

I lay there for a while, listening to a shuffled mix on my iPod. As a rule, I didn't listen to anything released after 1999, so every song that came on was pretty awesome. Midway through the chorus of "Smells Like Teen Spirit," I got the distinct impression that someone was watching me.

Wondering if maybe a cute boy really did live next door, I opened my eyes.

Gross.

Someone next door was watching me through the gaps in the fence, but he wasn't cute, or remotely close to boyhood. This gray-haired old dude was totally ogling me. When he saw me glaring at him, he immediately went back to pulling the weeds in his pathetic little garden. I guess his wife refused to do it. Good for her. If her man was eye-raping teenagers, he ought to be doing the hard labor. Pervert.

I got up and turned my chair around to face the other direction so the perv couldn't look at me. Any enthusiasm I'd felt earlier for tanning was pretty much gone. Having Nathan mentally undress me was one thing. I mean, I guess it was technically kind of weird, since we were going to be step-siblings, but at least he was my age, and hot — and with Nathan, I'd wanted him to do it. This dinosaur was just a creep.

I sat back in the chair and put on some Joan Jett. She always helped me work through my anger. I had this feeling that if we met in real life, Joan would have loved me. We were kindred spirits. If anyone could make me feel better, it was her.

It was scorching hot. I was barely clothed and still felt like I'd been put in an oven to bake. I squeezed my eyes shut again, deciding to think about something else. If I wanted a decent tan, I'd just have to deal.

I couldn't help thinking of the place where I should have been tanning. A big-ass lake with sunlight gleaming off the surface. A striped beach towel stretched out across hot sand. Surely there were disgusting old guys lurking around there, too, but I'd never caught them spying on me.

Everything about this place was wrong, like a fun-house mirror distorting the reflection of what my summer was sup-posed to be. On the surface, some parts looked the same; I was still with Dad, the way I wanted. But the details were altered beyond recognition. The people, the location, even this goddamn swimming pool — none of it was right.

I groaned and rolled onto my stomach, laying my iPod next to me on the lounge chair. The next song on my playlist was Bananarama's "Cruel Summer." How appropriate. This summer was more than cruel, though. It was a nightmare. And I just wanted to wake up.

Whit... Whit, wake up.

If only it were that easy. If only someone could just shake me a little. I wanted to open my eyes and be back at the condo, in the old bed with the creaking frame, wrapped in the neon-green and orange comforter Dad bought me the first summer we spent there, the smell of charcoal from the grill wafting in through my bedroom window.

A hand on my shoulder, sending me back there, shaking me out of this summer, this bad dream.

For a dazed moment, it was like God had heard my prayers. I felt a cool palm pressed against my bare back, nudging me gently.

It took a minute for reality to sink in, and my first coherent thought was that the gross old guy had hopped the fence and was trying to molest me or something. So I flailed onto my side, slapping at my attacker with the back of my hand.

"Aah! Shit," he groaned when I felt my class ring collide with some part of his face.

"Serves you right," I muttered.

"For what?"

I paused for a second, then rolled onto my back. It wasn't the creepy dude at all.

"Nathan? What the hell were you doing?"

"Trying to wake you up," he said, clutching his cheek. "You fell asleep. You've been out here for, like, two hours, and you were getting sunburned."

"What?"

I twisted my head around to look at the back of my shoulders. Red. Very red. I pressed a finger to my skin and watched as it turned white under the pressure. *Ouch.* I was seriously scorched, and only on my back, so I wasn't even icky red all the way around. Sunburns are bad, but uneven sunburns are the worst.

"Goddamn it."

"Come on. We have some aloe vera inside. It looks like you'll need it. You're a lobster."

"Shut up," I snapped. I jerked out my earbuds and stomped toward the back door with Nathan trailing behind me. He was laughing under his breath, and I thought about back-handing him again.

"Follow me," he instructed, moving in front of me and leading the way down the hall. Bailey was sitting on the couch watching the Disney Channel. Wasn't thirteen, like, way too old for that? She switched it off quickly when she heard us coming, and then turned around on the couch to look at me, her eyes widening. But before I could say anything, Nathan grinned at her. "Whit took a little nap outside. Isn't red her color?"

"Whitley!" I shouted.

Bailey tried to hide her giggles but failed. "Are you okay?" she asked me.

"No," I grunted. "Not at all."

I followed Nathan into the bathroom and waited as he pulled open the bottom cabinet. "I think Mom put it in here." After a second he found the bottle of green gel. "Here you go," he said, holding it out to me.

"Can you put it on my back?" I turned, pulling my hair over my shoulder.

"Uh…"

I glanced over my shoulder at him. He was eyeing me uneasily, his cheeks turning just the slightest bit pink. "Oh, please, Mr. Cool and Collected. Don't pick now to go all awkward on me. I'm not trying to seduce you or anything; I just can't reach it myself, and it's not like it's anything you haven't touched before."

He gave me a warning look.

"Right," I said. "I forgot. That never happened. Whatever."

Nathan sighed and flicked open the bottle. I turned my head and heard him squirt the gel into his hand. An instant shiver ran up my spine when his aloe-covered fingers hit my shoulder.

"Christ, that's cold," I gasped.

"Sorry."

My whole body tensed as his palm moved down the back of my arm. The chill started on the surface, but it seemed to move deeper. Invading my entire body.

71

It only got worse when he rubbed the gel between my shoulder blades and down my back. Nathan's hands were calloused, but not too rough. His skin passing over mine left a strange tingly sensation. Like an ice-cold fire spreading across my back and seeping into my veins. Even my fingers trembled a little, and I clenched my fists together to stop them.

"You okay?" he asked.

"Fine," I murmured, but I was on the edge of convulsing.

Every second Nathan's hands were on me, another moment from graduation night flooded back into my memory. The way his fingertips had pressed into my hips. The way I'd practically thrown him on the bed. The way he'd kissed me, more passionately than anyone else ever had. I remembered the half-crazed feeling when he took his time kissing me, touching me, whispering things in my ear.

Most boys take advantage of drunk girls. They make the sex all about them and their own pleasure. But that night with Nathan had been different. It had been slow and sweet. All about me. It had been amazing.

Suddenly, I realized the chills going through me weren't just from the aloe vera. Worse, I was the one blushing.

I felt the sudden urge to relive those almost-forgotten memories as his palms moved down my back. Part of me wanted him to untie the top of my bikini. His thumb slid slowly down my spine in a way that made my breath catch in my chest and my heartbeat speed up. Pounding faster and faster and faster. I was caught somewhere between wanting him and wanting to hide, feeling suddenly embarrassed and a little shy.

Nathan stopped. His hands were just above my waist. I held my breath, not wanting to move, to break the spell. Waiting to see what he'd do.

"You can reach the rest," he said, pulling his hands away from my skin so fast you might have thought I'd burned him. I know I heard his voice crack a little when he spoke. "You'll be able to get to your legs, right?"

"Um, ye-yeah," I stammered, not making eye contact as he handed me the bottle of aloe.

Nathan didn't say another word. He just slipped out of the bathroom, shutting the door behind him.

It had been fun pushing him this morning in the kitchen, but having the tables turned sucked. This whole stepsibling thing had just gotten infinitely worse.

8

"**Oh, honey,**" **Sylvia said, putting a hand on my arm when I came down for dinner that night.** "Your shoulders are so burned. Are you okay? Let me take a look."

I jerked away as she reached up to push my hair aside so she could see the back of my neck and shoulders. "Ouch. Don't touch. It's fine," I said, moving toward my chair.

Once I'd sat down, I looked back at her. Our eyes met for a long moment before Sylvia shook her head, sighing. "Okay. Well, I'm sure Nathan showed you the aloe vera we keep in the bathroom."

I nodded, forcing myself not to look at Nathan, who was sitting across the table from me. I was sure I could feel heat, unrelated to my sunburn, creeping up my neck.

"If you need anything else, let me know and I'll pick it up on my way home from work."

"Sure."

Bailey walked into the dining room just then, blond ponytail swinging like a pendulum behind her. She took her usual seat between Sylvia and me. "Is your sunburn feeling any better?" she asked.

I gritted my teeth. "It's fine."

When Dad entered the dining room I half expected him to comment on my fried arms and shoulders, which were totally exposed in my tank top. But he didn't say anything. He just sat down on the other side of me, barely glancing my way, and asked, "How did your first day of work go, sweetheart?"

"Really well," Sylvia said, scooping chili into a bowl and passing it to Bailey. "I really feel like I fit in there. Don't get me wrong — I liked the people at the other firm. But this one is smaller and more . . . friendly? I feel more comfortable there in one day than I ever felt at my old job."

"Do you get your own office now?" Bailey asked.

"Yep. I'll take you to work with me so you can see it if you want."

Bailey blushed. "Mom, you take your little kids to work — not your teenagers."

"I can take anyone I want." She handed me a bowl of chili, smiling. "You can come too, Whitley."

"Maybe," I muttered. *Or not.*

"What about you kids?" Dad asked, taking a sip of his tea. "Are you guys getting to know each other pretty well? I'm sure it's a little bit awkward at first."

"Yeah," I said. "I'd say we're getting to know each other *really* well. Wouldn't you, Nathan?"

He kicked me under the table and mouthed, *Not funny.*

Oblivious, Bailey added, "Whitley and I watched a movie today and hung out. We like the same kind of music — it was fun."

I nodded, even though I knew Bailey had only pretended to know the songs I'd listed for her when she quizzed me that afternoon. Not that many thirteen-year-olds were familiar with bands from the nineties. But she'd smiled and nodded and acted like she knew them all.

"That's great," Sylvia said. "What movie did you all watch?"

"*Bring It On.*"

"Again?" Sylvia laughed. "It's a miracle you haven't worn that DVD out from watching it so much."

Bailey ducked her head. "I can't help it."

"Speaking of movies." I turned and looked at Dad. "There's this new sci-fi film in theaters now. I saw the trailer on TV today. Do you want to go see it this weekend?"

"Sorry, munchkin. I can't this weekend," Dad said. "I have to give the commencement speech at a local university on Saturday. And I'm filling in for the evening news on Sunday — Tommy's got to catch a flight to Colorado for his sister's wedding and can't do the show. But I'm sure Nathan will drive you to the theater. Won't you, Nate?"

"Um, yeah. Of course."

"Great," Dad said. "You'll have to tell me how it is." He

76

stood, picking up his unfinished plate. "I hate to leave so soon, but I have to get back to writing this speech." He kissed Sylvia on the top of her head before leaving the room.

When the chili was eaten and the table cleared, Nathan and I headed upstairs to our rooms.

"When do you want to go see the movie?" he asked when we reached the landing. "Lucky for you, I'm a big fan of sci-fi."

"Yeah," I said quietly. "So is Dad. He's made me watch every *Star Wars* and *Star Trek* movie ever made at least once. Sometimes we'd stay up late having marathons — one right after the other."

"That sounds fun."

"I hate sci-fi."

"Wait — what?"

"I hate science fiction. I just watch it because Dad loves it." I let out a breath. "Don't worry about the movie Saturday. I'm not interested, so you're off the hook and we can go back to counting the days until we're away from each other."

I'd just pushed open the door to the guest room when Nathan asked, "Whitley, are you okay?"

I looked over my shoulder at him. "Do you care?"

"Yeah — of course."

"Why?"

Nathan raised an eyebrow at me.

I shook my head. "Never mind. It doesn't matter. I'm fine." Before he could say anything else, I walked into the guest room and shut the door.

"Yeah, I'm having a great time," I lied when Mom called on Wednesday.

"Are you and your dad spending much time together?" she asked.

She wasn't asking for my sake; I knew that. She wanted me to complain. She wanted an open invitation to bitch about him.

I didn't want to hear it.

"Um, yeah," I said. "He, um, wants to go mini-golfing this weekend." I forced a laugh. "How lame is that, right?"

"It sounds nice. . . . I was worried about you, you know."

No you weren't.

"Well, things have gotten better," I maintained. "I over-reacted the other night. It's not so bad, really. We've all been hanging out and watching movies. It's the same as always, just with a few more people in the house. It's great."

"Don't get used to it, sweetie," Mom warned. "Things are happy now, but your dad will mess it up. He always does."

"Whatever."

"I'm serious," she said. "I don't want you to be surprised or upset when it happens. It's bound to go downhill."

"Uh-huh." I took a swig from the Margaritaville Gold while she went on and on, the whole time insisting that telling me this was for my own good.

She didn't know what was good for me.

I wasn't sure anyone did.

Sylvia came home from work early on Friday afternoon.

"Are you girls ready to go?" she asked Bailey and me. We were watching *American Pie* on one of the movie channels in the living room. Or, at least, we had been. Bailey had switched off the TV as soon as Sylvia opened the front door. She must not be allowed to watch R-rated movies. Oops.

"Go where?" I asked.

"You didn't tell her, Bailey?"

Bailey looked sheepish. "I forgot. Sorry."

Sylvia shook her head, laughing a little. "It's okay. Well, Whitley, it looks like you're in for a fun surprise today. Come on. Let's go."

I had to be a bridesmaid.

That was the "fun surprise" that Sylvia sprang on me

twenty minutes later, when we pulled up in front of the bridal shop in Oak Hill, a city in the next county over from Hamilton. My summer was just full of awesome surprises.

"Oh, something like this would look great on you," said Sherri, Sylvia's just-as-blond, just-as-perky older sister.

She'd met Sylvia, Bailey, and me at Gwyneth's Bridal Boutique that afternoon, wearing a bright red blouse and sipping Starbucks coffee. She wasted no time in giving me a hug, telling me I was beautiful, and informing me that I was free to call her Aunt Sherri whenever I wanted.

I couldn't tell if she was a total phony or if she was just clueless.

I already disliked Sherri. Probably because she was so much like Sylvia. But right now she was making matters worse by holding up a sickening baby-blue dress, complete with puffy sleeves and a high neckline, saying how it was just right for me.

"Yeah," Sherri agreed with herself. "This would be excellent with your figure. And this shade is definitely a good color for you."

I couldn't help but think of what Harrison would say to this woman if he saw the horrible dress she was showing me. He'd flip his shit. Have an aneurysm. The sight of this thing might have even killed him. I know I wanted to die at that moment.

"Oh, Sherri, put that away!" Sylvia laughed from the other side of the small parlor. "You know Bailey and I already have the dress picked out. We just need to get Whitley's measurements."

"Fine." Sherri sighed. "But Whitley might still want to try on some of these, just for fun."

"No, I'm good," I said. "Really."

"Whitley, come look at the dress we've picked," Bailey said, waving me over. Given a choice between Bailey and Sherri, I chose Bailey immediately. I skirted around the racks of colorful gowns until I was standing next to the little blond and her mother. "Sorry about her," Bailey murmured. "Aunt Sherri gets excited easily." She cleared her throat. "So, this is it. This is the dress." She pointed to the one Sylvia was examining.

It was bubblegum pink — an instant reason to hate it — and floor-length. The sleeves came to mid-forearm and the bodice was decorated with a spray of tiny yellow fabric-and-bead flowers going up the middle and over one half of the sweetheart neckline. Exactly what you'd expect Sylvia to pick out for bridesmaids' dresses.

And exactly what I wouldn't be caught dead in.

"It still needs to be altered," Sylvia said, as if reading my mind. "I'm going to have the sleeves taken off and the hem shortened just a little. The wedding is in early September, so it will still practically be summer. I think that will look much better."

"What do you think?" Bailey asked.

"Gorgeous," I grumbled.

"Did someone need measurements?" called a woman from

81

the front desk just as a redheaded customer exited the boutique carrying a large frilly dress wrapped in plastic.

"Over here." Sylvia stepped out from behind the wall of hanging dresses. "One of my bridesmaids needs to be measured for her dress." She beamed before ushering me toward the desk, where the clerk waited. "This is Whitley. She's a bridesmaid for the Johnson-Caulfield wedding. You should have me on file."

"I do," the clerk said after a few seconds. "The pink gown with the flowered bodice, correct?"

"That's right."

"Great." She turned to me then. "All right, Whitley. I'm Lexie. Follow me back into the fitting room and we'll get your measurements done."

Lexie was one of those overwhelmingly pretty people. Not beautiful, but pretty. Stick thin. Black hair cut just below her chin. And she walked like a Victoria's Secret model, strutting down the runway. I couldn't help admiring her as she led me to the back room of the shop. This chick had it going on.

"Step in here," she said, gesturing to a dressing room hidden behind a white curtain.

"Why?" I asked. "I thought we were just doing measurements."

"We are," Lexie replied, picking up a strip of measuring tape from a nearby table. "But this is a form-fitting dress, and to get an accurate measurement, I'll need you to strip down to your underwear. Unless you're cool with everyone

82

seeing," she added, gesturing to the door as Sherri, Sylvia, and Bailey entered behind us.

I groaned and walked into the dressing room, Lexie on my heels.

Not that I had a problem with my body — for the most part, I didn't — but these were the last people I would want to see me in my purple bra and thong. They'd probably be scandalized by all that (currently sunburned) skin.

Though I really didn't want Sexy Lexie to see me practically naked, either. I could feel her eyes on my flat butt, my less-flat stomach. The smug expression on her face when I pulled off my T-shirt told me exactly what she was thinking:

I'm hotter than this chick.

Or maybe she was inwardly laughing at the blistering sunburn that covered the back side of my body. That was possible, too.

"Arms up," she said, unwinding the measuring tape.

I raised my arms above my head and winced as she wrapped the measuring tape around my chest, the edge of the strip cutting painfully into my inflamed skin.

"Might try a higher SPF next time," Lexie commented, moving the strip down to my midsection, not bothering to be any gentler, despite having noticed the burn.

"Yeah, thanks," I muttered. "I appreciate the advice. Because I had no idea what had gone wrong."

Outside the curtain, I could hear Sherri saying, "You know, Sylvia, you didn't have to take off work today. I could have brought the girls here on my own."

"I know," Sylvia replied. "But I wanted to spend a little time with Whitley. We barely know each other, and moments like this are a good way to bond." Even though she lowered her voice to a near whisper, I could still hear her add, "I just don't want her to hate me like I hated Alice, you know? I remember what it's like to have a crappy stepmom. I don't want her to go through that."

"Oh, honey, don't worry." Sherri laughed. "I don't think anyone could ever be as bad as Alice. Whitley will love you. Just give her some time."

Sylvia sighed. "God, I hope so."

"All done," Lexie said from behind me, her voice loud enough in my ear to make me jump. "You can put your clothes back on now."

"Great."

She slipped out through the curtain and told Sylvia she'd save the measurements in her file. The dresses would be ready in a few weeks.

After putting my cutoff shorts and T-shirt back on, I met the others in the main room of the boutique. Sylvia smiled at me. "You'll look so beautiful in the dress. I can't wait to see it on you."

I shrugged, then hesitated. I hated that Sylvia had changed my father. I hated that she was so freakishly happy when I wasn't. But as much as I wanted to spite her, to make her as miserable as I was, knowing that she was trying so hard made me feel just a little guilty.

I cleared my throat. "I mean...thank you."

A few minutes later, on our way out to the car, while Bailey babbled to Sherri about some new movie she wanted to see, I heard someone calling my name from across the parking lot. I turned and saw Harrison hurrying toward me, dressed in neat jeans and an emerald green polo that made his eyes pop — even from this distance.

God, he was gorgeous. The female population was seriously missing out.

"Hey, girl," he said when he caught up to me.

"What are you doing here?" I asked.

Beside me, Sylvia cleared her throat. Sherri and Bailey were already in Sherri's car (Bailey was going to spend the rest of the afternoon at her aunt's), but Sylvia had hung back, waiting to see who I was talking to, I guess. Nosy much?

I rolled my eyes. "Sylvia, this is Harrison. Harrison, this is Sylvia — Nathan's mom."

"Nice to meet you," he said, shaking her hand. "You're Greg's fiancée, right? You're a lucky woman."

"Thank you," she said. "I think so, too. And I'm glad to see Whitley is making friends here in Hamilton." She squeezed my shoulder and I cringed. "Oh! Sunburn — I forgot. Sorry. Well, I'll leave you two alone. It was nice meeting you, Harrison."

When she was across the parking lot and in the front seat of her Prius, Harrison said, "She seems nice."

"I guess. So, what are you doing here?"

"Oh, I work here."

"Here? At Gwyneth's?"

He nodded. "Yeah. It was a summer job turned all-year job once I decided to take the year off."

"Oh. Cool."

"It's nice — good experience for a fashion major and all that jazz." He sighed. "I just prefer men's clothing. You can only look at so many dresses a day, you know?"

I nodded. "Yeah — I know."

"So, are you still coming to the party tomorrow?" he asked.

"Is there still going to be booze?"

"Yes."

"Then yes."

He laughed and shook his head. "Well, I'm glad to hear it. Call me and I'll give you the address, okay?"

"Sure." I glanced over my shoulder at the car, where I could see Sylvia watching us from the window. "I should go."

"Me, too. See you tomorrow."

I turned and started to walk away, but before I got too far Harrison added, "And hey, be careful out in the sun. You're starting to resemble a tomato."

"*Yes*, I'm aware. Bye, Harrison."

When I got into the car, Sylvia had that toothy smile on her face. "He seems like a sweet boy," she said. "Did you meet him at the Nest the other night?"

"Yeah."

"Are you guys going to be hanging out?"

"Maybe."

"Oh, that's great. I'm so happy you're making friends. I was a little worried with how you'd adjust. New place, new people. I know it can be daunting. But Harrison seems like a nice boy to be friends with."

I let out a loud sigh, letting her know that the chitchat was getting annoying. "He's not my friend," I said flatly. Before she could ask questions, I leaned forward and fooled with the radio, stopping on the first classic rock station I found and turning up the volume. She didn't turn it back down, and she didn't push the subject.

10

"Are you going to a party?"

Bailey was standing in the doorway to the guest room that night, an hour or so after getting back from Sherri's house. I wasn't sure how long she'd been standing there. Long enough to hear at least part of the phone conversation I'd just had with Harrison. She smiled and walked inside, sitting down on the edge of the bed.

"Yeah," I said, putting my cell on top of the dresser.

"Can I come?"

I should have known that was coming. Bailey hadn't said much about her night at the Nest, even though I knew things hadn't been as exciting as she'd hoped. But apparently she hadn't given up on the Hamilton social scene just yet.

"I don't know."

"Please, Whitley?" she said. "I won't get in your way or

anything. I just . . . I don't want to be the only girl to start high school without knowing anyone, you know?"

"You're better off staying on your own," I told her. "Friends are a waste of time."

She frowned at me. "Why?"

"They just are," I said. "The kids in high school suck. They're selfish and fake. You're better off being a loner."

Bailey shook her head. "That's stupid," she insisted. "Maybe you're too much of a grouch to make friends, but I'm not, so —" She broke off, a little blush on her face. "Sorry. I didn't mean for that to sound so mean. But seriously, can I please go with you?"

I sighed. "Whatever. I guess you can come. The party's tomorrow night."

"Yes!" She bounced up and down on the bed a little. "How are we getting there?"

That was a good question. Harrison was riding over with some friends of his, so he couldn't pick me up; Dad probably wouldn't be back from the college he was doing the commencement speech for; and there was no way in hell I was asking Sylvia to take me. She'd probably ask to meet the host and bring a tray of cookies or something.

Which meant I only had one other option.

"Come in."

I pushed open Nathan's bedroom door and found him sitting at his desk.

"Oh. Hey, Whit."

He looked up from his laptop, sounding surprised. I wondered what he was doing on there. Looking at porn, maybe? That's what most eighteen-year-old boys used computers for, right? Somehow, though, Nathan didn't strike me as the type. Maybe it was the Spider-Man comforter on his bed or the Darth Vader bobblehead on his shelf, but he seemed to be more nerdy than pervy.

Not what I'd expected from the party animal I'd met graduation night.

"What's up?" he asked.

"I need a favor."

"What kind of favor?"

"Can you drive Bailey and me to a party tomorrow night?"

Nathan frowned. "I don't know...."

"What's the problem?" I asked. "It's not like you have an issue with parties."

His expression soured, and he looked at me with distaste.

"Get over it, Nathan," I snapped. "It happened. We screwed. I'm sure you don't want to piss off your mommy, but pretending you're a saint in front of me is pointless."

"I never said I was a saint."

"Then get the stick out of your ass and take Bailey and me to the party." When he still didn't move, I sighed. "Please? I want to go, and so does your sister. I just want to have a little fun, and I wouldn't be asking if I had any other options."

He chewed on the corner of his mouth for a second.

"Fine," he said at last. "But I'm coming, too. Someone's got to keep an eye on Bailey."

"She doesn't need a babysitter," I told him.

"She's thirteen. She's too young to go to a party without someone watching out for her."

"Then I'll keep an eye on her," I said, hoping to talk him out of actually coming to the party. I won't lie — part of me worried that if I got too drunk, I'd try to sleep with him again. Being at the same party with Nathan Caulfield just seemed like a recipe for disaster.

"All right," he said. "But I'm still coming."

I groaned. "Why?"

"I'll stay out of your hair. And I'll be the designated driver. I'd just feel better if I was there."

I wouldn't, I thought. But I knew there was no arguing with him. At least it would make Harrison happy. "Whatever."

"All right. Do you have an address for the place?"

"Yeah." I pulled the folded paper out of my pocket, the one I'd jotted Harrison's directions on, and tossed it to Nathan. "I want to be there by nine, okay?"

"You're the one who takes five years to get ready, remember?"

"Shut up."

I turned and started to walk out the door, but Nathan said, "Whit?"

"Whitley. And what?"

"Do me a favor. If Mom asks, we're going to see that sci-fi

movie and doing late-night bowling afterward." He looked at me seriously. "Don't tell her about the party."

"Fine by me."

I made a point of getting up early Saturday morning (as in, before noon) so I could see Dad before he left for the commencement ceremony. It didn't seem like we'd talked much at all that week. When he wasn't at work, he was busy hanging paintings or putting away some of the things still left in boxes from the move, or else he was glued to his laptop. The only times he wasn't busy were during dinner or when he sat down to watch ESPN with Nathan, neither of which were great opportunities to have a one-on-one conversation.

But Saturday morning, while Sylvia and Sherri went to do some wedding shopping and Nathan and Bailey were still asleep, I went downstairs to join Dad for breakfast.

"Hey, munchkin," he said when I walked into the dining room in my pajamas. "You're up shockingly early."

"Yeah." I walked through the archway into the kitchen, heading for the cabinet with the cereal bowls. "I thought maybe we could catch up before you left. We haven't really had a chance to talk much. How's work going?"

"Pretty well," he said, loudly so I could hear him. I poured some cereal and joined him at the dining table. "They offered me a job on the evening news a couple weeks ago because one of the anchors is moving to Dallas. The bosses think I'd up the ratings in that slot."

"Cool. Will you take it?"

"No." He took a sip of his coffee. "I like my schedule the way it is now. I get home around noon and Sylvia gets home at five. If I did the evening news, I'd be leaving right before she got home and getting in late. I'd never see her or the kids."

"Right," I said.

It was stupid to feel jealous. I knew that. I just wished I could see Dad every afternoon the way they would, instead of just a few months a year.

"What about you?" he asked. "Excited about college?"

"A little. Actually, I've been meaning to talk to you about that. I've been thinking about what I should major in, and I was wondering if you could —"

I was interrupted by the sound of the cordless phone ringing. Dad picked it up. "Hello? Oh, hey, sweetheart... Hold on. Let me look at the guest list. I was thinking we had two hundred people down, but that number might be off. Just a second." He covered the receiver. "Sorry, munchkin. I've got to help her with this and then get ready to hit the road. We'll talk college later, okay?"

"Yeah, sure. Later."

He ruffled my hair as he walked past me, out of the dining room.

I ate the rest of my breakfast alone.

11

Nathan had to park his Honda a whole block from the party, which was a good thing for two reasons. First, it gave Bailey and me the chance to ditch him before we even got to the house. I don't know about her, but I didn't want to be seen with the guy wearing a shirt that said, MAY THE MASS TIMES ACCELERATION BE WITH YOU. Second, it meant there were *tons* of people at this party. And hopefully tons of alcohol, too.

So, while Nathan locked up the car, Bailey and I made a run for it. Only we didn't really *run*, since we were both wearing less-than-abiding shoes (mine: platform slingbacks; hers: wedge heels), but we did manage to walk really, really fast. By the time we reached the front door of the party house — a total mansion, like Harrison had said — Nathan was far behind us. Well, he'd promised to stay out of our hair.

"Wow," I heard Bailey gasp as the front door swung open

for us, though I wasn't sure if that was her reaction to the freakishly large house or to the drop-dead-gorgeous guy standing in front of us.

"Good evening, ladies," he said, stepping aside to let us enter.

Automatically, I found myself standing up taller and sliding my shoulder blades back for optimum cleavage exposure. It was like a flirting reflex. I just wished I wasn't all sunburned. "Hello to you."

He grinned at me. A cocky, sexy grin. "I don't believe we've met," he said. He glanced at Bailey then. "Any of us. I'm sure I'd remember those pretty faces."

I swear, Bailey was blushing so hard I could *feel* the heat radiating from her body.

"Oh, you'd remember," I agreed, tossing back my hair and putting a hand on my hip. "I'm Whi —"

"Whitley!"

I jumped and spun around involuntarily. Harrison was standing beside me, looking thoroughly delighted. "Hello again, darling. You look gorgeous — and the lack of flip-flops is making my day. Those slingbacks are perfect!"

I nodded, glancing over my shoulder at the hot guy, but he'd already moved on and was chatting with a group of kids a few feet away. Goddamn it.

"Wesley is just so busy," Harrison said, following my gaze. "You have to give him credit for being a great host. He talks to *everyone*. Seems like way too much work to me."

"Yeah." I wasn't really listening. I decided I'd have to catch up with the guy later. He was my ticket to a good time. I'd just have to be careful not to drink so much I actually slept with him. Last time I let that happen, it hadn't exactly ended well.

Next to me, Bailey cleared her throat.

"Oh, um, Harrison," I said, snapping back to attention. "This is Bailey...my, uh, future stepsister or something."

Harrison's eyes lit up. "Nathan's baby sister? Oh, that's so sweet. Did your brother come with you?" he asked Bailey.

"Yeah. He drove."

"Oh, goody."

I rolled my eyes.

Harrison shrugged and smiled at Bailey again. "Great dress, by the way. Summer colors look amazing with your skin tone. So lucky you can pull off yellow."

"Oh...thanks," she said. "I got it on sale."

"Nice job," he said. "Okay, so...drinks?"

"Oh, Christ, yes," I said.

Bailey followed behind as Harrison and I made our way through the crowd toward the dining room. The place was packed with teenagers, and there didn't seem to be an adult in sight.

Harrison poured me a shot of tequila when we reached the kitchen. It was expensive tequila, much better than the stuff in my bedroom. I knocked it back in a heartbeat and set my glass on the counter, gesturing for Harrison to pour me another.

"Can I have one?" Bailey asked.

Harrison looked at me questioningly, and I shrugged.

"Here you go," Harrison said, handing a shot glass to her before pouring my second round.

I watched her bring the glass to her lips, sipping at the liquor a little at a time.

"Not like that," I told her. "You have to drink it all at once. Sipping at it like that will just make you miserable because it tastes like shit." Harrison held out my glass and I took it from him. "Like this." I downed it, the way I had the first, and put my glass back on the counter.

"Okay," she said. She took a deep breath and lifted the glass to her lips. I could almost hear her thoughts, counting down. *Three, two, one...* And then she drank it all. She sputtered a little, her face contorting at the taste, but she recovered pretty fast.

"There you go," I said, taking her glass.

"I...Can I have another one?"

"Don't overdo it just yet," I said. I thought for a moment, then picked up a glass, pouring her a little more tequila. This time, I half filled the cup, then mixed the alcohol with some fruit juice that had been left out. "Here. It won't taste wonderful, but you can sip on this for a while."

"Thanks," she said, taking the cup from me.

"Bailey," Harrison said. "You know, I have some friends who'd just adore you. Are you about to start high school? Freshman?"

She nodded.

"Fabulous." He winked at me and took Bailey by the

elbow. "Follow me, darling. There is a whole posse of sopho-more boys who would just eat up a cutie-pie like you."

She looked over her shoulder at me, grinning from ear to ear, as Harrison led her away.

"I'll catch up with you in a little bit," I told her. "Have fun."

I downed my third shot before mixing the juice and tequila for myself. Then I carried my glass back into the huge living room. The stereo was playing loud music — actually, it was pretty cool. Normally at this kind of party you heard the same rap shit. But this one seemed to be a little more upscale. Some really interesting piano rock boomed through the speakers, giving the place a more relaxed vibe. Of course, that meant no one was dancing. Honestly, though, that was probably a good thing.

With me, tequila combined with dancing often led to public stripteases.

I circled the room for a while, scanning the crowd that had congregated in the mansion. I recognized some faces from the Nest. Others were complete strangers. But it seemed like every type of person was at this party. Punks, emos, jocks, preps, geeks, and stoners. I wondered if every teenager in Hamilton was in this house.

About halfway through my third trip around the room, just as the tequila started to kick in, I spotted Wesley, the hot host. He was sitting on one of the couches, talking to some blond girl with a ponytail. When she stood up and walked away, I took my chance and dropped into the seat she'd abandoned.

"Hey," I said, crossing my legs and leaning a little toward him. "Nice party."

"Thank you. It took me forever to convince my parents to leave long enough for me to have something like this. But I figured a year away at college deserves a big welcome-home party."

"I think it does, too," I agreed. "Where do you go to college?"

"Columbia. I'm a business major."

"Wow. Smart and ambitious. That's a pretty big turn-on for girls, you know."

"That's what I'm told," he said. "Anyway, I'm sorry we didn't get a chance to talk earlier, and even sorrier I didn't get your name."

"Whitley." I didn't mention my surname. Last time I'd done that, the guy had totally admitted to crushing on my dad. No way was I letting that happen again. "And let me guess — you're Wesley, right?"

"That's right. Good guess."

"It was, huh?" I said, rubbing my lips together. "Hmm... In that case, I think I deserve a prize."

"A prize?" He laughed.

"Of course," I told him. "I totally deserve to be rewarded. On TV, when people guess the right answer, they get a prize. I want a prize, too." I scooted a little closer, my leg brushing his. "But I'd be glad to share. I'm not greedy."

He opened his mouth to say something, but before the

words came out, a girl collapsed onto the cushion on his other side.

"I hate parties," she growled.

Wesley turned his head to face her. She was short, with wavy auburn hair and a horrific sense of style. Her red Converse tennis shoes looked about six years old, and her T-shirt was so faded it looked like it would be a prime choice for a detergent commercial. Not the cool, store-bought faded, either. She needed a severe wardrobe check. Harrison would have had a field day with this girl.

"Hello there," Wesley said. To my surprise, he slipped an arm around her shoulders. "I see that it's working, then?"

"What is?" she asked.

"My strategy. The bigger the party gets, the sooner you'll retreat upstairs to my room, and then my victory can be secured."

She rolled her eyes as he placed a kiss at the junction between her shoulder and neck. "Perv."

He laughed. "Plus, you're hotter when you're annoyed." He looked back at me. "Whitley, this is my girlfriend, Bianca. Bianca, this is Whitley, the amazing name guesser."

Wait. His *girlfriend*? Seriously? In my experience, boys this hot rarely committed to anyone less than a supermodel. He was way out of this girl's league. Hell, Wesley was way out of *my* league.

"Well," she said, glancing at me, "it won't be long before I retreat if every girl here is going to insist on flirting with you."

"Can you blame them?" he asked.

"Of course I can. A smart girl would find your egomania repulsive."

"You know you like it."

"Maybe," she said. "But it took me a while. Your first impression? Not exactly charming."

"Hello to you, too," I muttered, even though I'd already been forgotten.

This was the second time I'd been shot down since arriving in Hamilton. Once because the boy was more interested in my dad, and now I'd been rejected for a girl in saggy jeans.

He kept his arm around her, and they started having a whole conversation that I was clearly not a part of. Names I didn't know. Places I'd never been. After a while, I stood up and left them on the couch. I wasn't drunk enough yet to think this was funny.

I didn't see Bailey when I pushed through the crowd. I thought about looking for her, since I'd promised Nathan I'd keep an eye on her, but after a second I decided against it. Nathan was being ridiculous and uptight. Bailey was probably having a great time, meeting kids from her school. She would hate me if I interrupted her fun or embarrassed her by checking in on her. Bailey was smart; she could handle herself. Smarter than I was at her age, anyway.

I poured myself another shot. Two more shots. Within ten minutes, I was smiling from ear to ear. Tequila made everything better.

"Hi."

I turned around and found a guy — kind of cute, nothing

special, but I wasn't picky — smiling at me. I grinned, putting my glass on the counter and leaning back against the cabinets. "Hey." I giggled. He had a nose like a pug's, and his hair was all spiky — it reminded me of a porcupine. "How are you?"

"Better now that I've met you."

Wow. That was lame. I snorted with laughter.

"So, what's your name?" he asked.

"Whitley."

"That's a sexy name."

"You bet your ass it is."

He smirked.

Five minutes later, the guy and I were going at it in a downstairs bedroom. Around the time his hand slid under my top, I realized I was really, really bad about getting boys' names.

I needed to work on that.

12

Less than twenty minutes later, I emerged from the bedroom with my hair in a state of total disaster. And all for nothing. About ten seconds after getting my shirt off, Pug Face had passed out on top of me. Ew.

At least that had kept me from sleeping with him. I knew I was drunk, but I wasn't sure if I was drunk enough to have let things go that far. Tequila always made me a little too agreeable, though. The thought made me giggle, but I wasn't sure how funny it really was.

I'd barely taken two steps into the living room, already on my way to get another drink, when Harrison appeared beside me, grabbing my elbow and yanking me off in another direction.

"Whoa!"

"Guys," Harrison said, dragging me along behind him. "Guys, okay, this is my new friend, Whitley."

Since when was I his friend?

"She's the one I told you about.... Greg Johnson's daughter."

I was being stared at by a mafia of skinny blonds. Well, okay, there was a redhead in the pack, but whatever. They all had on shiny lip gloss and nail polish, and each seemed to be carrying a different designer handbag.

"Did I just see you making out with Eric Higgins in the kitchen?" one of the girls asked.

"Was that his name?"

Even this drunk, I could see the way these girls looked at me. They stared down their perfect little noses, eyes narrowed in disgust. I knew these girls. They were the same everywhere. The rich bitches. The snobs. The girls who, my freshman year of high school, had convinced everyone — including my best friend — that I was a whore. Even by graduation, after all the parties and the boys, I still hadn't done half the things those girls claimed I had.

"Eric is kind of a weirdo," the redhead said.

"He's not a great kisser, either," I told her. "Too much tongue."

"Isn't she adorable?" Harrison said, squeezing my shoulders.

"Ouch. Watch the sunburn."

"Whoops. Sorry." He turned back to the girls. "She looks like him, doesn't she? Like her dad."

A few of the bitches nodded. The redhead was the first to

speak, though. For some ungodly reason — maybe because she was friends with Harrison, and he liked me — I half expected her to put aside the fact that I'd been making out with whatshisname, to give me a chance, to say, "Welcome to Hamilton. Where are you from?" I'd even have settled for, "Is your dad that tall in real life?"

Instead, she looked me up and down and said dryly, "Your shirt is on inside out."

"Yeah." I giggled, too giddy to be pissed. Plus, her lip gloss looked like clown makeup, and in that moment, it was the funniest thing ever. "I think it is."

The Blond Mafia just stared at me.

I turned to face Harrison. "M'kay. Well, I have a date with that bottle in the kitchen, so I'll see you —"

"Whitley!"

I paused, confused. Things were starting to get kind of hazy, and the fact that Harrison's lips weren't moving didn't make sense. How could he say my name if his lips weren't moving?

Then a very firm hand took hold of my upper arm, and I got it. Harrison hadn't been the one talking. Nathan was standing next to me now, squeezing my arm kind of hard. I stared up at him. "Sunburn," I whined, trying to jerk away. He loosened his grip but didn't let go.

"Oh, Nathan," Harrison said, smoothing his hair back with one hand. "Hi. Enjoying the party?"

"Not now, man," Nathan said harshly. He was glaring at me. "We're leaving, Whitley. Now."

"What? Why?"

He didn't answer. He just pulled me along after him as he began winding his way through the crowd. It wasn't until then that I really looked at him and realized that he had something large and bright yellow draped over his left shoulder.

Bailey.

Shit.

Her long blond hair tumbled down his back, and I could tell by the way she was lying, limp as a rag doll, that she'd passed out.

I stumbled behind Nathan, my platforms slipping from beneath my feet, but he didn't slow down. A few minutes later we were out in the humid night air. The rush of heat made me feel nauseous, but he just kept going.

"Wait, is she okay? Can we walk slower?" I complained as he pulled me down the sidewalk.

"I told you to watch her!"

He was yelling.

I laughed. Hearing him yell seemed so out of place. Cucumber-cool Nathan was yelling. It was hilarious. Like everything else about that night. Funny and hazy and strange.

"Damn it, Whitley, stop laughing," he growled, releasing my arm and turning to face me. He was holding on to Bailey's legs, her dress so short that I could see her pink underwear from where I stood. I wished he would change her position. That would embarrass the hell out of her if anyone saw. "You said you'd keep an eye on her," Nathan said. "You promised me."

"She's fine, though, right?" I said. "She just had a little too much to drink. I told her to take it slow."

"You shouldn't have let her drink to begin with!" he shouted. "She's *thirteen*, for God's sake."

"I had my first drink when I was fourteen," I retorted. "Not much older than her."

"Yeah, and look where it got you."

I froze for a second, stunned.

It took a minute for the words to sink in. I stared up at Nathan, anger burning away the amusement I'd felt before. Scorching the insides of my stomach and chest.

"Hypocrite," I spat. "I didn't hear you complaining last time we were at a party. You got wasted, too. It's not like I took advantage of you. You made the choice to sleep with me."

"I know," he said through clenched teeth. "And you were the biggest mistake I have *ever* made."

I drew back, my hand flying to my chest, my fingers curling into my palm. His words hit me like a punch in the gut. I opened my mouth to say something. To yell at him. To deliver a good comeback that would sting him in the same way. But nothing came to me. My throat was closing in on itself.

Biggest mistake. I was his biggest mistake.

He wasn't mine.

He didn't even make the top ten. Maybe not my top one hundred. Because, despite all of the shit going on, that night with him had actually been nice. Great, even.

Nathan's eyes softened, and he reached for me with his free hand. "Whit, I —"

"Don't touch me!" I screeched, slapping at his hand. "Get the hell away from me, Nathan."

"I shouldn't have said that. I'm sorry."

But I was already walking away from him.

"Whit, where are you going? Whitley?"

"I'm walking back."

"What? You're wasted. There is no way you can make it home on your own."

"Watch me."

And, as if to punctuate this statement, the back of my shoe slipped out from under me, sending me stumbling forward on the pavement. I caught myself by grabbing hold of a lamppost, but it took a second for me to regain my balance. By then, Nathan was standing beside me again.

"Come on, Whit."

"Don't touch me," I murmured. Tears were sticking to my eyelashes, and I was disgusted with myself. It wasn't just about Nathan; I knew that. I hadn't cried since arriving in Hamilton. I'd held back all the anger, all the hurt, everything I'd felt toward Mom and Dad and Sylvia. But being rejected by Wesley and kissing another boy I barely knew and wasn't even attracted to and the way the bitchy girls had looked at me and what Nathan had just said...It all piled on top of the hell I'd been through that week, and I couldn't keep it in any longer. But I hated myself for crying, especially in front of him.

Nothing was funny anymore.

"Come on," Nathan repeated. He didn't reach for me

again, but his eyes never wavered from my face. "Let's go home, okay?"

I took a deep breath and let it out slowly, blinking back the tears. Then I knelt down and slipped off my sandals. When I stood back up, I held them in my left hand, letting them dangle at my side. The sidewalk was dirty, but it felt cool and solid beneath my feet.

"Okay," I said, already walking toward the car. "Let's go."

Not home. It wasn't my home. But it would have to do for a while.

We didn't speak. Not a word. Nathan didn't even turn on the radio or sing or anything. In fact, the only sound in the car was Bailey's gentle breathing. She was asleep in the backseat of the Honda, letting out slow puffs of air through her nose.

My buzz was wearing off. I hadn't had quite enough to pass out — I had a high tolerance after so many years of this shit — but the headache was already coming on. You'd think the silence would have been a relief, but it made my head pound worse. I wanted Nathan to say something. Anything. Even if he was going to yell again, at least I'd know he wasn't ignoring me.

Anger was less painful than abandonment.

Anger, I could deal with.

I was so tied up in my own thoughts, trying to find a way to break the silence, that I didn't even realize we were pulling into a parking lot until the car came to a complete stop. I stared out the windshield at the darkened building. The sign on the door read FIFTH STREET FILMS — a movie rental shop. But it was closed for the night.

"What are we doing here?" I asked without thinking. Well, at least it wasn't silent anymore.

"They aren't asleep yet," Nathan mumbled.

"What?"

"Mom and Greg aren't asleep yet." He cut the engine, letting the headlights fade away. A single lamppost, twenty yards away, was the only light in the area, and it bathed us in a dim orangey glow. "It's only eleven. Mom is still up watching the news. It's not safe to sneak in until at least midnight. She thinks we're bowling, and the lanes close at twelve. So if we wait an hour, the coast should be clear."

"How do you —?"

"I've done this before," he said. "Remember?"

"Oh, right. I guess I just don't think about it. My mom would never notice if I came in drunk or something." I snorted. "And even if she did, she'd say it was Dad's fault, so I'd be in the clear."

There was a long pause, then Nathan said, "Um, you should fix your shirt before we go."

"What?" I looked down at my tank top. "Oh, right. Inside out."

"Yeah. Kind of a dead giveaway."

I reached down and pulled the hem of the shirt over my head. Once it was off, I glanced over at Nathan. He was facing the window, a hand clamped over his eyes. Even in the bad lighting, I could tell he was blushing. Christ. I had on a bra, and it wasn't like it was something he'd never seen before.

110

I slipped the shirt on the right way and said, "Okay. You can look now."

"Do you have any sense of modesty?" he asked, turning to face me. Maybe it was wishful thinking, but I thought I saw a small smile curling on his lips.

"Not after a few shots of tequila."

He didn't laugh as much as I hoped he would. It was really just an awkward half chuckle, but, hey, that was better than nothing.

He glanced into the backseat, and I followed his gaze. Bailey was curled into a ball, her knees pulled up beside her and her hair spread across the leather seat. To anyone else, it might have looked like she was sleeping peacefully, but to me it just didn't seem right.

"I'm sorry," I whispered. "I should have watched her."

"Yeah, you should have," he agreed. After a pause, he added, "I don't want her going to parties with you anymore, Whitley."

"Seriously, Nathan, you're overreacting."

"No, I'm not. You aren't the one who found her. You didn't see…" He took a deep breath, shaking his head slowly.

"What?"

"Nothing."

"No, tell me."

"Just drop it, Whitley. It's nothing. But she's not going to parties with you anymore." He took a breath and let some of the tension leave his body. "Look, you go to parties to escape — I get it. But if you're going to be this messed up,

111

that means you can't look after her, too, so you're on your own from now on. Okay?"

I sighed, rolling my eyes. I wasn't that messed up. Not yet. "Yeah. Whatever." I twisted around to face forward again. According to the clock on the dashboard, it was only 11:21. We still had more than half an hour to sit here, waiting to go back to Dad and Sylvia's house.

My headache was getting worse again. I leaned my temple against the window, closing my eyes. Since I could remember, I'd always been a night person. My burst of energy came right around the time the sun set. I lived in the darkness. Loved the darkness. My world came alive when the stars came out.

But for the first time in my life, I wanted the night to end.

I woke up the next morning to the sound of Bailey retching in the bathroom next door. That hangover was going to be hell.

I stayed in bed for a while, thinking about the night before. Poor Bailey. The first hangover was always the worst. I felt a little guilty for not giving her a better warning, for not keeping an eye on how much she'd had. At ninety pounds, it probably didn't take a lot to get the kid smashed. I hadn't even thought to tell her that.

Probably because no one had warned me about limits the first time I ever drank.

I hadn't been awake long when Sylvia found Bailey in the bathroom. I listened to their muffled voices, unable to make out the words. I heard them leave the bathroom and walk down the hallway, Sylvia's heels clacking past my room, the door to Bailey's room shutting a moment later.

I wondered if Sylvia would be able to tell Bailey had a hangover, or if she'd think the kid was just sick. If she knew it was a hangover, how much trouble would Bailey be in? How did someone like Sylvia punish her kids for drinking?

The truth was that I'd never actually been in trouble before. Not once.

Back when my parents were married, Mom had been the authoritarian. It was hard to imagine now, but she'd been tough on Trace and me as kids. Not that I needed any sort of discipline. Before the divorce, I'd been the good kid. Straight A's. Middle school student council. Perfect, perfect, perfect.

Obviously, that had changed.

But by the time I became a "bad kid" or whatever, Mom was too busy being angry at Dad or depressed about everything to care what I was doing. So I'd never been punished for the drinking or the parties or staying out too late.

Whatever happened between Sylvia and Bailey, it didn't involve yelling. The house was nearly silent for almost half an hour. Then I heard Bailey's door open and shut again, and Sylvia walked back up the hallway. Three light taps on the door across the hall. She'd moved on to Nathan.

I sighed and climbed out of bed, grabbing a pair of shorts and a T-shirt from my duffel. My own hangover was pretty minimal, since I'd stopped drinking around ten thirty. Most of the time, I didn't hit my stride until midnight or later. So I wasn't feeling half bad when I reached for the doorknob, intent on grabbing some breakfast downstairs.

At least I wasn't until Sylvia spotted me.

"Whitley," she said as soon as I walked out of my bedroom. She was sitting on Nathan's bed, staring at me through the open door. I could see Nathan on the other side of her, still in a T-shirt and pajama pants. He was facing the wall, so I couldn't see the expression on his face.

"Um, yeah?"

"Would you mind going back to your room and waiting for me?" she asked. "I need to have a talk with you."

Shit.

"Uh, sure. But will it take long? I'm really hungry and want to grab breakfast."

"It'll only take a second."

I nodded and slouched back into my room. This could not be good.

I sat down on the bed, twisting my hands together. Why was this worrying me? What the hell could Sylvia do? Nothing. She had no proof that I'd done anything wrong. That's what I told myself when she walked into the guest room five minutes later, anyway.

"Whitley." She sighed, not looking at me at first. "Whitley, Whitley..."

Yeah, that's my name, I thought. *Get to the point.*

I watched as she sat down in the chair in front of the desk, turning it to face me. "So..." she said, her eyes wandering the room. After a moment, they fell on my duffel bag. "You haven't unpacked yet?"

I shook my head.

"Why not?"

I shrugged.

"Oh...well, okay."

There was a long pause. She wasn't saying a word, just looking around the guest room and occasionally glancing at me. It was driving me nuts. So nuts I had to break the silence and get her to the point. Even if I was in trouble, that was better than letting her sit there screwing with me.

"Did you have something you wanted to talk about?"

"Yes."

I sighed loudly. "Well, I mean, like I said, I'm really hungry, so can we hurry this up?"

Sylvia shot me a sharp look, warning me to watch my step. At least I thought she did. The menace disappeared so fast I wasn't sure if I'd really seen it or not.

"Okay," she said. "It's about the party you kids went to last night when you told me you were out bowling."

So Nathan or Bailey had ratted. Lame.

"I'm very upset that my daughter — my *thirteen-year-old* daughter — was at a party and drinking, especially when I hadn't been informed." She paused, as if I should respond to this. I didn't, and she continued. "I don't condone that kind of behavior in my home, Whitley — or outside of it, if we're getting technical. Not from my children."

116

"Okay," I said. "So tell Bailey that."

"I've already spoken to both her and Nathan."

"Good to know."

After a mini staring contest, Sylvia started to shake her head. "Listen," she said. "I'm not your mother, or even your stepmother yet, but —"

"No," I agreed. "You aren't. I'm not your responsibility, and it isn't your place to punish me. You can't even prove I did anything wrong at the party."

"You let a teenage girl drink," she replied. "And I'm sure I can safely assume she wasn't the only one of you drinking. I'm a lawyer, Whitley. Don't challenge me to prove anything."

I rolled my eyes. "Whatever."

"And as long as you are living under my roof, spending time with *my* children, you are most definitely my responsibility. I've already discussed punishments with Nathan and Bailey. I'll be discussing yours with your father when he gets home."

"Gets home," I repeated. "Where is he now? He didn't have to cover Tommy's show until four."

"He had to run a few errands before work," she said.

"Right." I gritted my teeth, staring out the window. "Good luck discussing that punishment thing with him. Apparently, he's impossible to talk to alone for more than five seconds. Maybe he'll make the time for you, though."

"I know he's been busy this week," Sylvia said. "It must be hard not getting to talk to him, but —"

117

"No," I said. "What's hard is living with an embittered psycho twenty-four/seven and only seeing my dad once a freaking year. Then, when I finally do see him, he's too busy trying to make his new family happy to spend any time with me."

"That's not —"

"Don't tell me it's not true, Sylvia," I snapped. "Your freaking guest list was more important than talking to me about college yesterday. The first time we've talked alone since I got here, and you and your wedding had to ruin it."

I knew I was being selfish and overdramatic, but at that moment, I didn't care. If Sylvia was mad at me because of something as stupid as a party, I was allowed to be pissed at her, too. I thought she'd raise her voice, yell at me, tell me how ridiculous I was being, and that would have been fine. But she didn't.

"I'm sorry," she said.

I stood up and started toward the door. Sylvia reached out for me, but I pushed her hand away. I didn't want her to console me. I didn't want her to try to be a good stepmom. I just wanted her to go. Because if Dad weren't marrying her, none of this would be happening. I wouldn't have gone to that party, Bailey wouldn't have gotten drunk, and I wouldn't be in trouble now. If she had never met him, Dad and I would be having one of our great summers together right now.

Dad would still be mine.

"Look," I said to her when I reached the door. "Why don't you just figure out my punishment yourself and let me know.

Because Dad's just going to agree to whatever you want, anyway."

"Whitley..."

"I'm hungry," I said. "I'm getting breakfast. Just tell me what my punishment is when you figure it out."

I opened the door and ran downstairs as fast as I could, hoping she wouldn't follow me. She didn't.

Nathan was sitting at the dining room table, eating a Pop-Tart and using his laptop. "Good morning," he said without looking up.

"For who?" I walked into the kitchen and grabbed a bagel before heading back into the dining room. "I cannot believe you ratted us out."

"I didn't."

"So Bailey just admitted to your mother that not only did she get drunk, she also lied about where we were going?"

"She didn't have to. Mom's not an idiot, Whit."

"But you acted like you had it all figured out last night," I said.

"Yeah, well, that was before Bailey woke up with a massive hangover. Kind of obvious she didn't get that from the bowling alley."

"We still could have made something up," I argued. "We could have —"

"Look," Nathan said, finishing off his Pop-Tart. "Mom's not clueless. She can figure this stuff out. We couldn't have lied our way around this. Trust me."

I didn't question him any more. It was just weird to me,

119

the idea of someone who paid that much attention, someone who actually tried to see through the bullshit stories. Sylvia definitely wasn't like my mother.

"All right, kids." Sylvia appeared in the doorway of the dining room. "I'm going to the office to do some last-minute research for this trial. I shouldn't be gone long. Keep an eye on Bailey for me, please. Whitley..." She looked at me for a long moment, then shook her head. "You're grounded for the week, unless your father says otherwise."

Oh, well, I thought. *It's not like there's anything to do in this town, anyway.*

"Nathan, come on," she said. "I'll drive you to the gym on my way."

"Okay. Give me a second to grab my stuff."

She nodded and walked back into the living room.

"Why is she driving you?" I asked as Nathan crumpled his Pop-Tart wrapper.

"I lost car privileges for two weeks," he said. "I can't go anywhere unless she or Greg drives me. So, basically, I'm grounded."

It didn't seem fair that Nathan was being punished for two weeks when I only got one. Not that I felt sorry for him, but he really hadn't done anything wrong. Sure, he'd made up the lie, but he'd stayed sober and taken care of Bailey when I hadn't. I decided to keep my mouth shut, though. I should be grateful I got off easy by comparison.

"Why is she letting you go to the gym, then?" I asked.

"I have to stay in shape for basketball," he said, taking his trash and empty glass of milk into the kitchen. "The season doesn't start for a while, but it'll be easier to get back into the swing of things if I keep working out."

"I didn't know you played basketball," I said, nibbling on my bagel.

"You never came to a single game in high school?"

"If I did, I was usually hanging out under the bleachers."

Nathan sighed and walked back into the dining room. "Well, then, yes. I do play basketball. I got a scholarship to UK and everything."

I stopped chewing for a moment and stared at him. "UK?" I repeated. "You mean the University of Kentucky."

"Uh-huh."

As if this summer with Nathan weren't awkward enough, we would be going to the same college come late August. I tried to tell myself that UK was huge and the chances of us running into each other were probably slim, but I knew, I just *knew*, that wouldn't be the case. With my shitty luck, I'd probably have every class with him, or we'd live on the same floor.

"All right. I'm getting out of here."

I nodded, swallowing a piece of bagel. "Fine. Um, do you care if I use your computer? I'm kind of bored and wanted to surf the Web."

"No," Nathan said quickly. "I mean, yes, I do mind." He snapped the laptop shut and tucked it under his arm. "It's defragging, so it'll be a while before anyone can use it."

"Ooo-*kay*," I said. "Whatever."

It was so obvious he was lying. Maybe he *did* have porn on there.

"Right. Well, I'll see you later, Whit." He carried his laptop out of the dining room, leaving me sitting alone at the table.

After Sylvia and Nathan had gone and I finished eating, I went upstairs. I'd barely been in my room five seconds when my cell phone started to ring.

"Hey, Boozy!" Harrison said as soon as I picked up. "You hanging out with the toilet today?"

"Hardly. That was nothing last night," I said.

"Oh, really? God, I'd be afraid to see *something*, then. So what's up today, babe? Bonding with the stepbrother?"

"No," I said. "He went to the gym."

There was a long silence, and I heard Harrison let out a low sigh. I knew he must be imagining Nathan all sweaty and shirtless on the treadmill... or the exercise bike... with those lean, muscled arms and...

Christ, now I was thinking about it, too. Not a good idea.

"So," I said, clearing my throat. "What's up?"

"Not much. Just wondering if you had plans today."

"Nope."

"Want to hang out?"

"I can't," I said. "Grounded for the week. I'm not allowed to leave the house."

"That blows."

"I know."

"Hmm." He paused, then said, "Well, are you allowed to have people over to visit?"

"I'm not sure," I said. "I wasn't told *not* to. So..."

"Fabulous. I'll be at your place in twenty."

14

Sometime between Wesley's party and the Father's Day cookout Sylvia planned, Harrison Carlyle and I became friends. At least, that's what he claimed we were. I wasn't sure how I felt about it.

Don't get me wrong. Harrison was fun to be around. He'd come over almost every day during the week I was grounded (just as I'd predicted, Dad hadn't altered Sylvia's punishment). We watched movies and swam and talked about college plans. I had to give him credit; he kept me entertained, and Sylvia never said a word about me having guests over. If it weren't for Harrison, I might have gone crazy.

Still, once my sentence was over and Harrison and I began venturing out of the house, I wasn't totally comfortable with the way he introduced me as "my friend Whitley" or the way he'd laugh when we were talking and say things like, "I've never had a friend quite like you." I wasn't really sure how to contradict him, though, since I did like having him around — which is more than I can say about most people.

We spent time together almost every day, and when I told him about Sylvia's big cookout plans, he offered to crash the party to keep me from stabbing myself in the eye with a shish kebab rod. A party devoted to celebrating a father I'd barely spoken to in weeks, thrown by the people who'd taken him away? Since getting hammered wasn't an option, I knew I'd need Harrison's support.

We sat at the dining room table playing Crazy Eights — possibly the lamest card game in the world — while everyone else milled around the backyard with their hot dogs and red cups full of lemonade. Sylvia had invited all of her coworkers and their families, plus the other anchors from Channel 34. The turnout was pretty decent, I guess, but I couldn't help thinking that I should be spending Father's Day with my father, not with everyone he and his fiancée knew, and not with Harrison.

"You guys should come outside," Sylvia said, poking her head into the dining room. "It's a beautiful day, and everyone would love to meet you."

"We're fine," I said, slapping the eight of spades down on the pile and watching Harrison groan. "It's too hot out there, anyway."

"All right." She sighed. "But I hope you change your mind."

A minute later I heard her slip through the screen door in the kitchen, back to where her guests waited.

"I don't know why she won't leave me alone," I mumbled. "She's always breathing down my neck. Checking on me, asking if I need anything, wanting to know if I'm okay. I feel like I barely get a second to breathe."

"She's being nice." Harrison laughed, drawing from the deck of cards. "It's cute."

"It's annoying."

"At least she cares."

I remembered what Sylvia had said to Sherri at the bridal shop about being a better stepmom than the one she'd had growing up. "Yeah," I said. "I guess."

"Oh, you know what I just thought of?" he said. "You should stay over at my house soon. We could totally have a slumber party."

"Don't you think your mother would have a problem with a girl spending the night?" I asked.

"My mom knows I'm gay," he said. "She's fine with girls. Especially when I make new friends. She tries to fit in and be cool. It's kind of sad. So, will you stay over? We could watch movies and talk about boys and do all that fun stuff."

Was that stuff still fun? I didn't remember. I hadn't been to a slumber party since seventh grade.

"I don't know, Harrison."

"*Please.*"

I frowned and tossed an ace of diamonds onto the pile.

"Fine," I said. "Let's make a deal: You throw a party, let me get wasted, and I'll stay at your house that night."

"God, Whitley. You're practically auditioning for a starring role on *Intervention*."

"What?" I grinned at him. "I'm more fun when I'm drunk, anyway. Give me enough to drink, and I might even let you give me a makeover."

He laughed. "Okay. It's a deal," he said. "I'll just have to trick my mother into leaving the house for the night."

"Will she freak about the party?"

"Hell no." He snorted. "She'll want to hang out with us. And I wouldn't be able to survive that kind of social humiliation."

So it was settled. Harrison decided he would hold the party/sleepover on the Fourth of July, just over two weeks away. He could get his older sister to buy the alcohol, and his mother would be on a holiday retreat with some girlfriends. Perfect.

We'd finished our game of Crazy Eights and had moved on to Go Fish when Bailey walked into the dining room.

"Hey, Whitley," she said, hanging in the archway that connected the dining room to the kitchen. "Mom wants to know if you and Harrison want cheeseburgers. Greg is firing up the grill again."

"No thanks," I said.

"I'll take one." Harrison smiled at her. "You ungrounded yet, sweetie?"

She nodded. It had been two weeks since Wesley's party,

which meant her punishment was finally over. Not that she seemed particularly excited about it the way I'd expected her to be. She'd taken the grounding without complaint, and not once had I heard her express a desire to go anywhere once it was over.

Actually, since that party, Bailey hadn't been as chatty, at least not with me. It was really starting to freak me out.

I watched her disappear into the kitchen and out the back door. "Harrison, who were the boys you introduced Bailey to at the party?"

He shrugged. "Just some sophomore kids. I don't know them that well, but one of the boys was my friend Kelsey's younger brother. You met Kelsey at the party. She's skinny, blond."

"Oh, one of the Blond Mafia?"

"Is that what you call them?"

"Yeah."

Harrison laughed. "I like it. . . . Got any twos?"

I shook my head. "Go fish."

That night, I decided to give Trace a call. We hadn't spoken in weeks, and texting wasn't enough. I'd been ignoring Mom's calls for a while, unable to listen to her bitching, and I needed to talk to someone on the outside of this little bubble I'd been living in.

"I miss you, too," Trace said, sounding agitated. "Whitley, can I call you back later?"

"Um, sure, I just thought —"

"Emily's expecting a phone call about a job and our call waiting isn't working and if I tie up the line she might have an aneurysm. I'll give you a call later tonight if you want."

"No. It's fine," I told him. "Really. I'll call another time."

"Great. Love you. Bye."

The next day, Bailey asked me to help her practice for cheerleading tryouts. I wasn't sure how I, the anti-cheerleader, could help, but whatever. I sat on the front steps and watched as she did cartwheels across the grass and belted out goofy little rhymes.

"How am I doing?" she asked after about an hour of this.

"Good, I guess."

"*Good* isn't good enough." She sighed.

"It's just cheerleading."

"But it's important. If I want to be noticed in high school, I need to get this right."

"Christ, Bailey, you watch too much TV," I said. "That is *so* not how it works. You can be noticed for a lot of different things in high school. You don't have to wave a pom-pom for people to know your name."

"Did people know your name in high school?" she asked.

"Some of them. But I went to a big high school."

"How did you get noticed?"

I bit my lip. That wasn't a question I particularly wanted to answer. Not in detail, at least. "I partied a lot," I said. "So people started recognizing me."

"That won't work for me," she said. "I don't think I like parties."

129

"There are other ways, too. And being noticed isn't all that important. Trust me, sometimes it's better if no one knows your name."

She shook her head, as if I had no idea what the hell I was talking about.

"Fine," I said. "Keep doing your backflips or whatever. But for the record, I don't think you'll have any trouble getting noticed. People noticed you at that party, didn't they?"

She stared down at her feet. "I guess."

"See? Your life won't end if you don't make the cheerleading squad."

"I know." She tugged on the hem of her T-shirt and cleared her throat. "But will you help me work on this more tomorrow?"

"We'll see." I got to my feet. "You coming to the Nest tonight? To celebrate being ungrounded?"

"No."

"Why not?"

"I don't feel like it." Bailey opened the front door, and I slipped inside after her. "There's a movie coming on the Disney Channel tonight I want to see. But you and Harrison have fun without me."

"You sure?"

She nodded.

"Suit yourself, then," I said, though I was a little worried about her as I watched her walk into the kitchen. I knew the last party hadn't ended on the best note, but after being cooped up for so long, I thought she'd at least jump at the opportunity to listen to bad music and drink soda with Harrison and me. I guess I'd be mad at me, too, after the hangover she had, topped by two weeks of grounding. Was it weird that I was missing the old Bailey?

I walked upstairs and made my way down the hall toward the bathroom. I needed to get a shower before Harrison showed up. What would I wear? Hanging out with Mr. Fashion had me worried about my clothes all the time now. Maybe a pair of denim shorts with heels? I decided to confer with Harrison when he arrived.

I was so wrapped up in thoughts of my wardrobe that I didn't even think twice about pushing open the bathroom door.

Of course, as my luck would have it, the room wasn't empty.

"Hey!"

I was staring at a very wet, very naked Nathan, fresh from the shower and without a scrap of clothing covering him. Water dripped from his hair and gleamed on his shoulders... his broad, muscular shoulders. Those gym visits were definitely working.

"Oh, Christ," I gasped. I pulled myself out of the bathroom as fast as I could, but it didn't keep me from seeing *everything*. The door slammed behind me, and I hurried to the guest room, trying to shake off the weird daze.

Technically, I'd seen Nathan naked before.

I'd just forgotten how hot he was.

I ran my hands through my hair as I paced — pointlessly,

I might add — around the guest room. Nathan and I had barely spoken since the morning after Wesley's party. Dinners were civil but stiff. I was sure he was still mad at me about Bailey and the drinking, and I was busy seething about what he said that night and the fact that we'd be going to school together in the fall, not to mention trying to forget I'd slept with him.

There was no way I could forget now.

Graduation night, which had come back to me in bits and pieces, flashed through my mind again, as it had more and more over the last few weeks. His breath mingling with mine, his lips by my ear, his hands on my skin. Dear God, his hands made me go crazy. They had that night, and they had when he'd helped me put on the aloe vera a few weeks ago.

I shook my head. I had to stop thinking about this. I tried to think of something else, something disgusting. Anything that would be a major turnoff.

Like dead kittens.

Or spinach.

Yeah. None of that worked.

And it only got worse a few seconds later when the door swung open and Nathan — still wet, but with a pair of blue jeans covering his lower half, at least — walked into the guest room. The door clicked shut behind him. I could only assume he didn't want anyone overhearing whatever he was about to say.

"You know," he said, "you could knock."

Well, that was kind of anticlimactic.

"Well, you could lock the door."

God, I wished he'd thought to put on a shirt.

He rolled his eyes. "Look, there are three of us sharing a bathroom now. I know it's probably hard to get used to, but it'll make both our lives infinitely less awkward if you would just be the slightest bit consider —"

"Whatever," I interrupted. "Are you done in there? I need a shower."

He sighed. "Yes. I'm done in the bathroom."

"Good."

I walked past him as he turned around. We both reached for the doorknob at the same time, his hand landing right on top of mine as I moved to twist it. I looked up at him to say something mean, to insult him, to express my annoyance in some way — the things I did best.

He was looking down at me, his hair still soaking wet, his shoulders still glossy.

Hormones.

They're real troublemakers.

Before I even knew what I was doing, I had Nathan pinned to the wall, both our hands letting go of the doorknob at once. I didn't even realize I was kissing him until I felt his tongue slide between my lips. Well, at least this wasn't one-sided.

His hands were all over me. I pressed myself against him, my fingers twisting in his drenched hair. He was a better kisser than I remembered. Graduation night had been great, but I quickly figured out that sobriety improved Nathan's performance.

He was fiercer this time, too. Before, he'd been slow and

hesitant, but this time Nathan took control. It wasn't long before he started urging me backward, toward the bed. He pushed me onto the blankets, moving on top of me an instant later. It was very aggressive — insanely hot, but not what I'd expected from Nathan.

He kissed me hungrily, his lips occasionally moving to my neck to give me a chance to breathe. Cool water dripped from his hair and skin, soaking into my T-shirt. It was the most excitement I'd had all summer.

And then, just like that, it was over.

He was off me. Off the bed. Before I could even sit up, Nathan was all the way across the room.

"What's wrong?" I asked, breathless.

"Whitley, we can't do this."

"Why not?"

"You *know* why not." ·

Yeah, I did, but I didn't want to think about that.

Seriously, though, something had to be wrong with him. He totally could have had me, *again*, and he was just going to walk away. What the hell? No normal eighteen-year-old boy would do that... right?

"Are you gay?" I asked.

He snorted. "No."

"You sure?" I pressed. "Because if you are, Harrison would totally be willing to give you a shot."

"I'm not gay, Whit."

"Then what the hell is your problem?" I demanded, my voice cracking more than it should have. "Don't you want to?"

134

"I want to," he said, reaching for the doorknob. "But I'm not selfish enough or stupid enough to do that again."

"What is *that* supposed to mean?"

Nathan just shook his head. Then he was gone, closing the door firmly behind him.

That night at the Nest, I made out with a guy who had dreadlocks.

I thought I would hook up with him. I planned to. But we'd barely made it to the backseat of his car when I pushed him off me and said I had to go. I'd forgotten something. I had to be somewhere. And I left him, shirtless and swearing, in the car.

The truth was, the whole time Dreadlocks was kissing me, I was thinking of Nathan. I couldn't get his voice out of my head, or the taste of him off my lips.

But he wasn't selfish enough or stupid enough to sleep with me again.

Whatever he'd meant by that, it had stung.

I woke up at ten o'clock the next morning to the sound of someone banging on the door of the guest room. "Come in," I moaned sleepily.

"It's locked."

Oh, yeah. I'd forgotten about that.

For the past few weeks, Sylvia had been popping her head in every morning before she left for work. She never said anything, but the sound of the knob turning always brought me out of sleep. Harrison might say it was sweet of her to check on me, but I hated being woken up every morning at eight. So I'd started locking the door.

But now I didn't want to get out of bed to unlock it.

"Who is it?"

"Nathan."

"Go away."

"Let me in, Whitley."

I frowned into my pillow. He was calling me by my proper name, which meant it was something serious.

"Go away," I tried again. He was the last person I wanted to see. "I'm sleeping."

"Let me in!" Something hard slammed into the door, jolting me upright in surprise. Was he, like, punching it or something? "I'm not kidding, Whitley."

What the hell?

"Fine!" I snapped, falling out of bed and stumbling to my feet. "I'm coming, I'm coming." I walked across the room, flipped the lock, and opened the door, not even caring that my pajamas were skimpy and made of sheer material or that I hadn't put on a bra yet. That was his problem.

Lucky for me, though, he was fully clothed.

"What?" I demanded.

His eyes moved down my body for a second, and I didn't miss the way they lingered — for a fraction of an instant, really — on my chest. Christ, all boys were the same. It wasn't even like boobs were interesting. That was one thing I would never understand.

Still, even if he had rejected me last night, it was nice to know he thought I was attractive.

Nathan cleared his throat and shook his head. "Have you seen Facebook?"

"Um, no," I said. "I don't use Facebook. There's no point unless there are people you actually want to talk to."

"Come on." He grabbed my wrist and yanked me out of

137

the guest room, practically dragging me across the hallway and into his room. Then he shoved me into his desk chair and gestured to his computer screen. "Look."

Whitley Johnson: Hamilton's New Free Ride

The headline at the top of the page was the first thing I saw. Directly beneath it, in smaller text, was a short paragraph.

In late May, Hamilton welcomed the daughter of hottie anchorman Greg Johnson to town, but Whitley Johnson doesn't seem to be her daddy's sweet little angel. Looks like we've got a bad girl on our hands. What dirty antics will she get into next? If you spot her out and about (and we're sure you will), keep us posted!

"What the fuck is this?"

"A Facebook group," Nathan said.

"Why would someone make a group about me?" I asked.

"It's Facebook. You can make a group about the tree in your front yard if you want," he said. "Did you see the picture?"

I scrolled down. On the left-hand side I saw the page's main photo — a blurry shot of me, clearly drunk, stumbling around at Wesley's party. In the center of the screen, a little farther down, I saw the most recent post. It was marked as a mobile upload, a shot of me and the dreadlocks guy from last night. We were making out in a booth at the Nest, his hand under my shirt.

"Oh my God," I whispered.

"Keep scrolling."

I did.

There were more photos, taken with people's cell phones. Most of them were of me dancing with boys at the Nest, but a few were from Wesley's party — including an image of me taking a shot in the kitchen, Harrison at my side.

But the comments were the worst part.

What a skank. Could her skirt be any shorter in that pic?

Her dad seems so wholesome and sweet on TV. I bet he is soooo ashamed of her. Poor guy.

Man, I hope she's at the next party I go to. I'd tap that.

"Why would people do this?" I asked. I'd been called a skank and a slut and a whore and every other thing you could imagine before, but it had never been on the Internet. No one had cared enough to build a freaking web page.

"Your dad is a celebrity to these people," Nathan said. "Which means you are, too."

I clicked on one of the photos. Below the image was a list of people tagged. Greg Johnson was at the top of the list. My dad would see this picture of a boy with his hand up my shirt. Maybe he could see all of these photos.

"I can't believe this."

"Small towns are known for their big rumors," he said.

"And you're starting quite a few. Can you blame them for talking? Look at how you..."

"How I what?"

I was on my feet, my fists clenched. I felt like someone had read my diary — you know, if I kept a stupid diary — or like I'd just discovered a Peeping Tom. It was disgusting and embarrassing. I felt hurt, violated. And I just couldn't take Nathan acting like a prick on top of everything else.

"How I what?" I demanded again.

"How you *live*!"

"How I live?"

"You're wasted every chance you get — I saw the bottle of tequila in your room! You're selfish and careless. I mean, seriously? Screwing that guy right after we —"

"I didn't *screw* him," I interrupted. "We just kissed. And by the way, you're the one who put a stop to things yesterday, not me. So don't even act like that's an issue here."

"No," Nathan growled. "The issue is that you're acting like a whore and a drunk, and you need to cut it out."

I shouldn't have been surprised. He'd almost called me a whore once before, after Wesley's party, and like I said, it wasn't as if I'd never been called those names before. Still, hearing Nathan, someone I'd let touch me, someone I'd *enjoyed* touching me, put me down that way — it stung. More than I thought it would.

"It's none of your business what I do," I informed him.

"Actually, Whitley, it is. Because you're part of my family now, whether you like it or not. We've been through enough shit. I don't need you screwing things up even more. And this?" He pointed at the monitor, like I should look at the pictures again, like the images weren't already imprinted on my brain. "This is the example you're setting for my sister. She looks up to you, for some unknown reason, and this is what you show her. I don't want her turning out like you. You're the reason she drank that night. And you weren't watching her, so..."

There was a long pause.

He cleared his throat again, shaking his head.

"What?"

"Nothing."

I moved forward. "Nathan," I whispered. "What happened at that party? She's been acting weird ever since then. Please tell me."

He looked away, pressing his lips together and taking a breath before he answered. "When I found her, she was passed out in a chair. Two boys were with her, and one was... He was trying to feel her up while they laughed and egged each other on, like it was some joke." He shook his head again. "I stopped them, and nothing else happened. But something could have. Can you imagine what that would have done to her?"

Yes, I could. I could imagine it all too well.

I could *remember* it all too well.

"Does she know?" I asked.

"Not about how I found her. She remembers one of them kissing her.... She told me..." I saw his fists clench. "Her

141

first kiss was with some horny, half-drunk moron. Great memory for her. Something to tell her grandkids."

"Oh, God, poor Bailey," I murmured, guilt twisting my insides. I was supposed to have kept an eye on her.

"And it's because of you," he spat. "What else would she do when you throw yourself at every guy you see? And now with this fucking Facebook page!"

I took one breath, two, three...

"Get out of my way."

"What?"

"Let me out of here." I shoved him aside, needing to escape. My heart was racing, my head spinning. I just kept thinking of Bailey, of those boys....

"Don't you have anything to say?" he asked when I reached the door.

"Not to you."

I ran to the guest room, slamming the door behind me. I didn't let myself cry until I knew he wasn't coming after me.

16

I spent the next several days avoiding Nathan as much as was humanly possible. This involved lots of the silent treatment and cold-shouldering, mixed with a little bit of immature "Did you hear something? Must have been the wind," whenever he tried to get my attention in the presence of others. Sylvia raised her eyebrows at this once or twice, but she had the sense not to ask me questions. And Dad... Well, I didn't see Dad much, so he probably had no idea.

Bailey was the only one who ventured into the questioning territory, stupid kid.

"Did Nathan, like, do something to piss you off?" she asked one afternoon on the couch after Nathan spent ten minutes trying to talk to me with no luck.

"Since when do you say *piss*?" I asked, picking up the remote and flipping to a movie channel.

"I'm almost fourteen. I swear sometimes."

"I've never heard you swear."

"Well, I do. So, what did Nathan do?"

"Your mother will kill you if she hears you talking like that."

"I won't let her hear me, then," she said. "Why are you mad at Nathan?"

I groaned and leaned my head against the back of the couch. "Not that it's any of your business, but he said something stupid, so yes, I'm pissed at him."

"Oh. What did he say?"

I narrowed my eyes at her. "Bailey."

"Okay, sorry. I'll stop asking questions." She repositioned herself on the couch to see the screen better. "But you can tell me if you decide you want to talk about it."

"I'll keep that in mind, thanks."

Not many people could get away with pestering me the way Bailey did, but I was just incapable of getting mad at her. Maybe it was all the time we'd been spending together, watching bad reality TV and goofy eighties movies, or maybe it was the constant guilt I felt when I looked at her, thinking of what those boys had done to her and knowing it was my fault for not watching her.

Either way, I just couldn't get mad at her, even when she was at her most annoying.

"Hey, girls," Dad said as he walked into the living room.

He'd been doing something in his office ever since he got home from work earlier that afternoon. "Can you two do me a favor?"

"Sure," I said, twisting to look at him over the back of the couch. "What's up?"

"Do you mind picking up around the house? Taking out the trash, dusting some of the furniture, the usual? Sylvia's asked me to run to the grocery store, and I want the house cleaned up before she gets home."

"We can do that," Bailey said, switching off the TV.

"Thanks. I owe you both." He started for the door, pausing to slip on his shoes.

"Hey, Dad?" I said, getting to my feet.

"Uh-huh?"

He kept facing the wall, bending down to tie his shoes without looking at me. I wanted him to look at me, wanted to see his eyes when they met mine. He hadn't said a word about the pictures on Facebook, but he had to have seen them . . . right?

"Um, do you think we could hang out soon?" I asked. "To talk about, like, college and majors and stuff?"

"Sure. I'll have to look at my schedule, but I should have time next weekend. We'll do something then."

He had to find time in his schedule to talk to me. Wow, that made me feel important.

"Great," I said. "I'm going to spend the night at Harrison's on the Fourth, but maybe that afternoon? Before he picks me up?"

"Sounds good." He gave me a quick smile before pulling

open the front door and heading out. He'd glanced at me, but only for a millisecond — not enough for me to tell if he was looking at me differently.

I sighed and ran a hand through my hair.

"You okay?" Bailey asked. I turned and found her already holding a dust rag in her hand. "You look... Are you pissed at Greg, too?"

"Stop saying pissed. It's weird."

She grinned. "That time I just did it to see what you'd say."

I grabbed the dust rag out of her hand and started cleaning the entertainment center. "Go take out the trash, Potty Mouth."

She laughed and headed into the kitchen. "Pissed!" she shouted as she walked through the dining room. "Shit! Damn!"

I rolled my eyes. If Nathan heard her tossing out curses, he'd probably blame me for that, too. Say it was my influence or something.

Really, though, I wouldn't have cared. I was just happy she was in a good mood, laughing and joking. I was glad those boys hadn't taken that Bailey away from me. Especially because at the moment, she was the only person in this family I actually liked.

I got up early the morning of Harrison's party, hoping to spend a few hours talking with Dad about potential majors. I was fully prepared for an awkward confrontation about the Facebook pictures, and I'd even figured out exactly how I'd respond when he started asking me about the group.

Unfortunately, I never got the chance to use my speech.

I waited around downstairs all afternoon for Dad to get home from work. One o'clock, two o'clock, three o'clock... Around three thirty he called the house from his cell phone.

"Hi, munchkin," he said. "Could you do me a favor and ask Nathan to meet me at the theater? I'd swing by and pick him up, but it took longer than I expected to pick out fireworks for tonight."

"The theater?" I repeated. "Nathan? But I thought you and I were going to talk about college and...I don't know. Hang out."

"Oh, right," he said. "I'm sorry — I forgot. We'll do it soon, I promise."

There was some muffled noise from his end.

"I've got to go, munchkin," he said. "I'm in line to buy these fireworks. I'll see you tonight."

"I'm going to Harrison's tonight."

"Then I'll see you tomorrow," he said. "I love you. Bye."

I clenched my fist around the cordless phone for a long moment before slamming it back down on the counter. Frustration boiled inside my chest. He'd ditched me for Nathan. For his new son. His new family.

I turned and stormed upstairs, pushing open the door to Nathan's room without knocking. He was sitting on his bed, reading a book. He looked up when I walked in. To my surprise — and annoyance — he looked happy to see me.

"Hey," he said. "I'm glad you're here. I wanted to talk to you about what I said —"

"Dad wants you to meet him at the theater," I said. "He can't pick you up because he's buying fireworks.... You're going to the movies with him?"

"Um ... Yeah, I am. We're going to see that sci-fi movie — this is the last week it's showing. Is that okay? Do you want to come with us?"

"No," I snapped. "No, it's not okay. He was supposed to hang out with me today. He was supposed to talk to *me*. About my future, my major, the shit people are saying online. He hasn't talked to me about any of it, and he was supposed to today. But he's not. Instead he's going to the movies with you. And no, Nathan, I don't fucking want to come with you."

"I'm sorry," he said. "I didn't know. Maybe he forgot."

"Just like he's been forgetting to look me in the eye lately. No, he's just more excited to start fresh with his new, perfect family."

Nathan had the grace to look genuinely sympathetic, at least. "Is there anything I can do? I could cancel, or I could drive you, and you could go instead."

I softened a little. It was hard to be angry when he seemed to really care — even if my dad was replacing me with him. "No. I just — I need to check something on your computer."

"Um, okay. What?"

"Facebook." I sat down at the desk and brought up the Internet. I heard the springs of Nathan's bed creak as he set his book aside and walked up behind me.

"You don't want —"

"Don't tell me what I want, Nathan."

148

He was already signed in to Facebook when I opened the page. Finding the group wasn't hard. It popped up as soon as I typed my name into the search bar.

I scrolled down, trying to ignore the left panel and the *167 people like this* message there. Jesus, were there even 167 people in Hamilton to begin with? There were no new photos up, which made sense, since I hadn't left the house in the last few days. But posts and comments and speculations about where I'd been had popped up.

Rehab already, maybe?

Wonder if Greg shipped her back to where she came from? I wouldn't want my fans to see my daughter if she behaved that way.

I pushed their words out of my head and made myself click on the top photo — the one of me and the dreadlocks guy kissing.

"Nathan," I said. "If someone's name is tagged in a photo on here one day, but it isn't now … What does that mean?"

"The person tagged can untag themselves," he said. "Why?"

"Because," I said, "Dad was tagged in this photo when you showed me the page, and now he isn't. Which means he untagged himself. So he saw this picture. He saw it, and he didn't say anything to me about it. He just … He untagged himself. Like it never happened."

"Maybe he just —"

"He just doesn't give a shit."

I stood up and started for the door, but Nathan caught my arm. "Whit."

"Whitley."

"I'm sorry for what I said to you that day." Nathan's hand slid from my elbow to my wrist. "It wasn't okay for me to call you a whore. It's not okay for anyone to say that. Not the people online, and definitely not me. You told me once that I'm a hypocrite. And you're right. I am. You should know that I —"

"While I'm sure this is going to be a fascinating story," I interrupted, "I don't care. I'm having a major parental crisis that sort of outshines your little tantrum, and frankly it seems like my dad agrees with you. I have a party to get ready for, so can we do this later?"

He let go of my arm. "I get it. Yeah. Fine."

"Great. Thanks."

I knew this was Dad's fault, that it was Dad I should be angry with, but I hated Nathan right then, too. Because Dad was spending time with Nathan today instead of with me. Nathan was the child he wanted. He couldn't even make time in his schedule to talk to me, to care.

Untagged. He'd untagged himself from the photo.

From me.

17

"I think you've had enough, sweetie."

Harrison tried to take the glass from me, but I jerked away from him, keeping it out of his grip and spilling some of the vodka on my purple top at the same time. I hated vodka, but that's what Harrison's sister had bought for us. Whatever. It was better than nothing. Way better than yucky beer.

"Leave me alone," I said.

"You're smashed. And not in your usual goofy, funny way. You're getting obnoxious, and more than a little morose. You should stop now."

"I'm fine," I snapped. "It's the Fourth of July. I can have as much as I want. Mind your own business."

"God, Whitley, stop being so dramatic," he called as I walked away from him, crossing his backyard in a beeline for the row of trees.

I wondered if he'd seen the Facebook page.

I took another gulp of the vodka. I was still thinking about the Facebook page, about Dad. I was still thinking, so I wasn't drunk enough.

My hair was all in my face, and I tried to flip the strands out of my eyes somewhat gracefully. Thank God Harrison lived way out in the country. His house was set almost a mile off the highway, surrounded by thick woods. This was a fabulous thing since, apparently, he was incredibly popular. There had to be a hundred kids at this party. Every member of the Blond Mafia. Wesley and his stupid, ugly girlfriend. Geeks, jocks, preps. People in high school and on summer break from college. Harrison knew everyone.

I knew that these people had their little cameras ready, ready to catch me doing something skanky or illegal. I'd thought about it as soon as I arrived at the party. And then I thought, *Fuck it*, because Dad didn't care, so why should I? Might as well give these people the show they wanted.

But I flinched each time I saw someone on their phone, wondering if they were about to sneak a picture of me.

So I drank more, and waited for the moment when I'd stop caring.

I stumbled over a patch of uneven ground and my drink flew out of my hand, sending shards of glass scattering across the grass and turning the dirt into vodka-flavored mud.

"Shit," I whined, trying to correct my posture. I got a little assistance when a hand took hold of my elbow and helped me straighten up.

"Steady there."

"Thanks," I muttered.

"Not a problem."

I turned to face my rescuer. He had blond hair, a strong jaw, and really shiny teeth. Maybe it was just the drunk goggles clouding my vision, but at that moment, he looked like perfection in the flesh.

"Hi," I said, smiling. Behind him, the backyard blurred and tilted.

"Hey," he said, still holding my elbow. "You're Whitley, right?"

I grimaced. "How did you know?"

"Harrison told me about you," he said. "His sister and I go to college together. My name is Theo."

I was relieved to know that he knew me from Harrison rather than from the Facebook page. For a second, I was worried he was one of the 167 people who'd joined the group.

"Theo," I said. "That's an interesting name."

"So is Whitley." He grinned, leaning in to whisper in my ear. "But I like it."

A chill ran up my spine. "Do you?" I murmured.

"It's sexy."

I laughed. "Theo... Your name makes me think of Alvin and the Chipmunks."

He chuckled, pulling back from me and letting go of my arm. "Well," he said, "I guess I'll leave you alone. You probably want to hang out with your friends."

I scoffed. "What friends?"

153

Theo gestured to the crowds all around us. They were a fog of brightly colored clothes and swaying limbs. No faces. No familiar or distinct voices. Everything blended together. Strange and unreal.

But Theo was right in front of me. Solid. Clear.

"They're not my friends," I said, stepping closer. "I'd rather spend time with you."

"Me?" He raised an eyebrow. "An old college guy? I'd probably bore you to death."

"I wouldn't mind."

His arm was around my waist. I wasn't sure how it got there. "Then maybe you've just made a new friend, Whitley Johnson."

I shook my head, but that only made it hurt. "Nah," I said. "I don't do friends. But we can hang out."

"That works for me."

So Theo and I sat on one of the picnic tables, away from the rest of the partygoers, and just talked for a while. He was a music major. He liked Elvis, Jet Li, and extra-cheesy pizza. He knew the names of every constellation in the sky that night, and he didn't mention my father once.

By one AM, I was smitten.

But by two, he was standing up, moving away from the picnic table.

"Where are you going?" I asked, trying to follow him and tripping over my own feet. I'd had two more glasses of vodka and Sprite since we'd started talking.

He smiled at me. "I just have to run to my car," he said. "I

154

left my cell phone out there, and I should probably make sure my mom hasn't tried to call."

"Your mom?"

"Yeah." He shrugged, apparently a little embarrassed. "She gets a little protective when I'm home for the summer. It's sweet."

"Moms don't like me."

"My mom would." He grinned and turned around again, walking toward the front yard.

"Can I come with you?" I asked, stumbling after him.

"Of course," he said, his hand quickly sliding around my waist, helping me to keep pace and remain upright. "You're great company. I just feel bad for keeping you from all the other kids your age."

"First of all," I slurred, "I'm not a kid. And secondly, I like you better. They're dumb. You're fun."

"And you're just drunk enough to actually believe that." He laughed. "I'm boring, I swear."

"No, you're not. You're cute."

We were walking around Harrison's house now, nearing the front yard. The sounds of the party faded into the distance behind us as we moved toward the driveway and Theo directed me to his SUV.

I snorted. "My dad drives one just like that."

Theo chuckled. "Your dad must have good taste. This baby is amazing."

"Boys who like cars are lame."

"Hey," he said, pulling open the driver's side door, "you're the one who thinks I'm cute. So, technically, that makes you pretty lame, too."

"Shut up."

I glanced through the window as he pulled his cell phone from the console. Leather interior. All shiny and pretty. Everything was exactly like Dad's...except for the stereo.

"Dude!" I cried. "Your stereo kicks ass!"

"Girls who like stereos are lame," Theo teased.

"I thought I told you to shut up."

"Never said I'd listen."

I made my way around the front of the car and climbed into the passenger's seat. "Play me something," I demanded, leaning back. "I want to see just how awesome that thing must sound. What did you pay for it? Two hundred bucks?"

"With the new speakers, it was closer to five hundred," he said, sitting down in the driver's seat and shutting the door. The windows were rolled up. The party was far, far away. We were all alone.

"What are you in the mood to hear?" he asked, hooking his MP3 player into the system.

"Michael Jackson," I said.

Theo raised an eyebrow at me. "Really? You like MJ?"

"Yep. Can you guess my favorite song?"

"Easy," he said. " 'Billie Jean.' "

"You got it."

He smiled and pushed a few buttons on his MP3 player. Seconds later, Michael Jackson was singing to us about the beauty queen who was *not* the mother of his baby.

"You know, Whitley," Theo said, his lips suddenly very close to my ear, "you're pretty cute for a high school girl."

"I'm not in high school," I told him. "I just graduated, thank you very much. I'm going to be a freshman in college soon. Maybe I'll major in music, like you. But I'm a big girl now, no kid."

He chuckled again. He had a cute chuckle.

"That's good," he said. "Then I don't feel so guilty about doing this."

Then he was kissing me, and I was kissing him back. He had very strong lips. They sent shock waves down my spine. My arms wrapped around him, and my eyes slid closed. The windows were tinted; there would be no pictures of this online. No small-town paparazzi. This was all mine.

But for some reason I just couldn't get into it. Theo was a good kisser, and he was attractive, but the longer it went on, the less I wanted it.

"Hey...stop," I gasped, pulling away as Theo's hand slid beneath the waistband of my jeans. "Slow down, okay?"

He pressed his mouth against mine again, but his hands didn't stop. His fingers kept dancing down into my jeans, toying with the elastic of my underwear.

Part of me wanted to say *Screw it!* and let him do what he wanted. Why not? It wouldn't be the first time I'd slept with someone I barely knew, and I came into tonight looking for some level of hookup. It's not like anyone would think less of me.

But maybe *I'd* think less of me . . .

I kept imagining Nathan. Showing me that stupid website.

157

Reminding me of the example I was setting for Bailey. Saying he couldn't believe I'd sleep with someone after we...He hadn't finished that thought.

"Seriously," I murmured, pushing at Theo's wrist. "Not tonight."

Theo's hand slid out of my pants and I relaxed. Until he began trying to pull down the zipper of my jeans. When I pushed at his wrist again he resisted, shoving me lower in the seat as he moved in closer. My head thudded against the passenger's window and my back pressed into the door, the handle digging into my spine. Theo's face, distorted and hazy, swam before me. Then it — he — descended on me, like a snake striking its prey.

All of a sudden, I was scared.

"Theo, quit it," I said, firmly this time. Or at least I tried to sound firm. I knew my words were slurring, and I could feel my voice shaking when I spoke. "I'm not joking."

"Shh," he whispered in my ear. "You know you want to. I'm cute, remember? Way cuter than that guy in the photo. With the shitty dreadlocks."

I felt something catch in my throat.

He had seen the Facebook page.

His mouth covered mine, but it felt more like suffocation than a kiss. I pushed at his arm again, trying to turn my head so I could breathe. But his whole body was on top of mine now, holding me in place. When his tongue forced its way between my lips, I bit down as hard as I could.

Theo jerked back, and for a second I thought I was free. I

groped for the door handle, but then he lunged at me again, knocking my searching hand aside and hitting the lock on the door. I was drunk and he was fast. He had my wrists, forcing them over my head.

"Stop!" I screamed. "Stop! *Stop!*"

But the windows were rolled up. The party was far, far away. My phone was somewhere out there. We were all alone.

And if someone happened to walk by, to stumble upon us, they wouldn't stop him. They would think I'd asked for this. They'd think I *wanted* this. Or maybe they'd think I deserved it. My antics, my "behavior," had finally gotten me into serious trouble. Would they believe that? Because of a stupid website and a few stupid kisses and more than a few stupid drinks — would they believe I'd set myself up for this?

Maybe I did. Maybe they'd be right. Maybe this was my punishment for hooking up with boys I didn't know, or for drinking so much I couldn't fight back.

"Please don't," I said, sobbing, tears rolling down my cheeks as Theo made another move to push my jeans down.

"Get the fuck off her!"

The driver's side door was yanked wide open. Two hands caught Theo's shoulders and dragged him away from me.

With my arms released from his grip, I grabbed the waistband of my thong and jeans and yanked them back up, closing the zipper as fast as I could. I wanted to lock them, if that was possible. To make it so that only I could unfasten my pants. No one else.

It took me a minute to find my breath, but once I could

inhale and exhale normally again, I unlocked the door and hurled myself out of the SUV.

I couldn't stand up anymore. My legs gave way, and I fell on all fours, puking next to the passenger's side door of Theo's SUV. Face wet, throat aching, I practically crawled around the front of the vehicle, trying to figure out what had just happened.

Then I saw Harrison.

His fists moved so fast that I barely saw them, but I heard the thuds as each hit Theo — one in the jaw, one in the stomach.

The last thing I saw before I passed out in the gravel driveway was Harrison's foot colliding with Theo's rib cage as he lay, groaning, in the grass.

Yes, I thought as the blackness swept over me. *Harrison is definitely my friend.*

18

When I felt the fingers brushing through my hair, my first instinct was to jerk away. My eyes snapped open, my hand swatting blindly. Theo's perfect face and shiny teeth flashed in my mind. Only, now they looked much less attractive. The strong muscles in his jaw were menacing, and the glittery teeth were sharp and dangerous.

"No!" I gasped, rolling onto my side. But I wasn't in the SUV anymore. Or lying in the driveway. It took me a second to realize that the ground beneath me was soft. There was even a pillow propping my head up.

"Shh...Whitley, it's okay."

My eyes found Harrison's, and a sigh of relief exploded from my lips.

"Thank you," I murmured, trying to sit up. "Thank you, thank you, thank you."

He put a hand on my shoulder, forcing me to lie back down. "Don't get up yet, okay? Nathan is on his way."

"What?"

"I called him."

"Forget those thank-yous."

I didn't want Nathan to see me like this. I didn't want him to know how badly I'd screwed up this time, how right he'd been about me. That I was a drunk and a whore. This was my fault, just like what had happened to Bailey was my fault. I didn't want him to see that he'd been right.

"He's coming to take you home," Harrison said, sitting down next to me on the bed. I figured we must be in his room. The clock on the wall said it was just after three, which meant I hadn't been out for long.

"But what about our slumber party?" I asked.

"It can wait," he said, squeezing my hand. "You should go home tonight, sweetie."

"I'd rather stay here." But I knew I wouldn't be good company for the fun sleepover I'd promised him.

"We'll have a real slumber party before the summer's over," he said. "Just not tonight."

I rolled onto my back again, looking over at Harrison. "So, how did you find us?" I asked. "Theo and me... How did you know to look for us?"

"I found your purse on the picnic table," he said. "And my sister said she saw you hanging out with Theo. He's not a good guy, Whitley. He's my sister's on-again, off-again thing, but they pretend to be friends when they're off. It's weird...."

162

Anyway, he's a jerk. I got worried. So I checked the front of the house and I heard you yelling, and there you were."

"There we were," I whispered.

"Are you okay?"

"Fine," I said. "I'm just really, really drunk."

"Took you long enough to admit it."

"Screw you."

"You wish you could."

I laughed, but it hurt my head, so I stopped. "Ow..."

Harrison smiled. He placed his large hands gently on my shoulders and pulled me upright. "Easy," he murmured, just as the doorbell rang in the next room.

"You should get back to the party," I said when he slid an arm around me, walking me into the living room. "I'm making you be a bad host."

"Party's over," he said. "I kicked everyone out after I carried you inside."

"Christ." I dropped my head. "I'm so sorry. I totally ruined your party."

He squeezed my shoulder as we reached the front door. "Don't be sorry," he said. "I didn't give a shit about the party. I only threw it because you wanted me to. You're what I care about."

I smiled and clumsily kissed his cheek. "Why do you have to be gay?"

"That's just how God made me." He reached out with his free hand and opened the door, already wearing his flirty smile. "Hey there."

Nathan was standing on the front porch, dressed in the same battered blue jeans and black T-shirt he'd had on that morning. His hair was messier than usual, which meant he'd been asleep when Harrison called.

"Whitley..."

His dark eyes passed carefully over me, as if he was checking to make sure every part was still intact. When he looked into my face a moment later, he seemed relieved...and kind of sad. The expression reminded me of one Sylvia used right before she tried to hug me, and for a second I expected Nathan to extend his arms and pull me to him.

But he restrained himself. Instead, he turned to Harrison and said, "Thank you so much for calling me."

"Get her home safe," Harrison said, easing me onto the porch. I stumbled a little, and Nathan reached out to hold me up the way Harrison had.

"I can walk," I told them, though that obviously wasn't true.

"She's very drunk," Harrison said. "She had a lot of vodka."

Nathan sighed. "Okay. Thanks, Harrison. You know, she's lucky to have you. Anyone would be."

Why were they talking about me like I wasn't there?

Harrison grinned. "*You* can have me anytime," he said.

The way Nathan laughed made it clear that he thought Harrison was joking. But of course I knew he wasn't. Poor Harrison would never have a chance with Nathan. But still, I was grateful to him for keeping it light tonight.

"See you later," Nathan said, hauling me down the front steps toward his Honda.

"Bye!" Harrison called after us. "Be careful. Good night, Whitley. Call me if you need me."

"I will," I tried to yell, but it came out more like a croak as my knees began to shake beneath my weight.

"Careful," Nathan said, holding me up as he opened the passenger's side door. He helped me inside and made sure I got my seat belt buckled before shutting the door. He smelled fresh as he leaned across me, a little spicy, and his messy hair tickled my neck. I held my breath until I was buckled in. A second later, he slid into the driver's seat and turned the key in the ignition.

"Are you okay?" he asked, his voice so low that I barely heard it over the sound of the purring engine.

"Fine."

I saw his mouth open, like he might say something, but he shut it again, very slowly. The car began moving, turning around in the gravel driveway and rolling down the long, winding path to the highway with a slightly rocky bounce. Nathan stared out the windshield, his eyes never darting in my direction. He didn't know what to say, either, I guess.

I rolled my head to the other side and stared out the window. We were away from the trees now, and fireworks were shattering the darkness all around us. They'd probably be going all night, scattering temporary multicolored stars across the sky. Pinks. Blues. Greens. Reds. I was surprised they didn't give me a headache. I actually found them kind of peaceful in a weird way.

"Don't take me back," I whispered, the words leaving my mouth before I even realized I was going to say them.

"What?"

"Don't take me to the house." My eyes stayed focused on the fireworks. Bottle rockets flew up out of someone's backyard. "Can we go somewhere else?"

"Um...sure. Where do you want to go?"

"Anywhere."

After a moment, Nathan just said, "Okay."

"Where are we?" I asked as Nathan pulled the Honda into an unfamiliar parking lot. The building in front of us looked old and shabby. SHAY'S DINER was written on a lopsided sign above a cracked glass door. The windows glowed with a painful fluorescent light that made my head pound.

"It's the only place I could find open this late," Nathan said.

He unfastened his seat belt and climbed out of the car. With a sigh, I did the same.

"You said anywhere," he reminded me as he took hold of my elbow and helped me walk inside.

"Guess I did," I mumbled.

The place had those annoying bells that jingled every time someone walked in or out the door, and the waitress behind the counter called, "Hey, y'all!" the second she heard them. Like it was an automatic response. What a sad job to have. Greeting insomniacs at three in the morning with a stupid fake Southern accent. Not to mention the humiliation

166

of wearing that horrific apron. I kind of felt bad for this chick.

"Good morning," Nathan said, all friendly and cheerful. What a dork. "Can I get a coffee, please? Black. And a couple pieces of toast."

"No problem, sweetheart." She probably loved boys like Nathan. So polite and courteous. Of course, at this time of night, any guy who didn't smack her ass must have seemed like a godsend.

He walked me to a booth with a sticky table and slid into the seat across from me. A second later, the waitress appeared and placed a mug and a plate of toast in front of Nathan. She was in her mid-forties, with reddish-brown hair and a round face. She looked so warm and sunny. Not the kind of woman you'd expect to meet at a dirty diner in the wee hours of the night.

"There you are, baby," she said to Nathan. "You just holler if you need anything else."

Okay. So, maybe her accent wasn't fake. She sounded Texan, or maybe Alabamian. I could never tell the difference.

"Thank you," he said.

"Anything for you, honey?" she asked me.

I shook my head and curled into a ball where I sat, my feet in the booth, knees to my chest. I could still feel Theo's hands on my hips, his breath on my face. Like a ghost. Gone, but not gone.

"All right. Just let me know." She walked back to the

counter, her hips swaying to the beat of the country song that played from the ancient-looking jukebox in the corner.

I glanced around. Other than the waitress, Nathan and I were the only people in the diner.

"I guess Hamilton doesn't have many night owls."

"It must not," he agreed. "Here. Drink and eat this." He shoved the toast and mug toward me.

"Ew," I said, shoving the coffee back across the table. "No. I hate coffee." I didn't mind toast, though, so I picked up a piece and took a bite.

He rolled his eyes. "Come on, Whit, just drink it. It'll help you sober up. Well, okay, scientifically it won't, but I swear, it'll make you *feel* soberer. The toast will help, but —"

"I don't want to."

"Don't be such a baby."

"I'm not a baby," I snapped. We glared at each other for a long moment before I gave in and took the mug from him. To be honest, I was really, sickly drunk, and anything that might make me feel better was welcome...even if it *did* taste like shit.

"You've got to be kidding me." Nathan laughed as I lifted a hand to pinch my nose. "Are you six years old or what?"

"Shut up." I took a deep breath through my mouth and raised the mug to my lips. It was scalding hot, and the nose-holding thing didn't do much to mask the coffee's bitter taste. It took all of my strength to swallow a few gulps without spitting it out.

When I put the mug back down, Nathan grinned at me.

"I hate you."

"You just wish you did," he said.

I took another drink of coffee and picked up my piece of toast again.

"The face you make when you drink it is hilarious," he teased.

I swallowed a slightly burned bite of bread. "If you aren't careful, I'll spit the next mouthful all over you," I warned.

He laughed again, but it faded into silence within seconds. His face turned suddenly serious, and I braced myself, arms around my knees again. I knew what was on his mind. It was on mine, too. But I didn't want to talk about it. Or think about it. Ever again.

"Please, don't," I said when he started to open his mouth. "Not right now, okay? I can't talk about it right now. . . . Can we talk about anything but that?"

"Fine. But if you need to —"

"I know."

"Okay."

"Okay. Talk about something else."

There was a long pause, then Nathan finally said, "I'm sorry."

I stared at him, a little confused.

"I told you this afternoon, but you wouldn't listen," he said. "I mean it, though. What I said —"

I shook my head. "Don't bother. It wasn't like you were lying, after all."

"But —"

"It's fine," I said. "It's just...ironic."

"What do you mean?"

"Back home in Indiana, when I was hooking up all the time with random guys, people called me a whore, but it was like... It wasn't like everyone knew my name. But here? I've been *good* in comparison to what I used to do. I haven't done anything with anyone but make out, yet everyone cares, everyone knows me. They call me a slut, but since I've been here, I haven't even done anything."

Nathan looked a little surprised. "You mean, you aren't... You didn't...?"

"Nope. The last time I got laid was graduation night," I said. "And that wasn't really a normal thing."

"What do you mean?" he asked. He was sitting sideways in the booth, one leg hanging out into the aisle between the tables. He was playing with the hole in the knee of his jeans, his eyes on his fingers, like he was suddenly very interested in the denim. "How wasn't it, uh, normal?"

"I don't have sex with everyone," I said. "I've hooked up a lot. But I could count the number of people I've slept with on one hand, including you. You'd never know it based on what people say, or those pictures, but..."

"Oh."

I leaned back in my seat and stared out the dirty window. A few fireworks were still erupting from a church parking lot across the street.

"Weeks of posts, tons of comments, pictures he was

tagged in...and my dad hasn't said a word. He just untags himself."

"That's why you do this, isn't it? Because of your dad?"

I turned to face Nathan again. "What do you mean?"

"Your dad," he said. "Okay, this is going to sound really shrinkish, but I think you act like this — party, drink — because you want his attention. Don't you?"

"No. That's stupid."

"Really?" He leaned across the table, his eyes on mine. I looked away, and he asked, "Then why?"

"Why what?"

"Why do you do it? Go out and get wasted all the time. Why?"

My first feeling was anger. I wanted to yell at Nathan and tell him that I lived this way because I wanted to. Because it was fun. Because it worked for me. But that was bullshit. Especially after what had happened tonight.

This wasn't fun. It hadn't been for a long time.

I thought of Bailey. I'd been so much like Bailey once. Somehow, I'd gone from that to...this.

"Remember when I told you that I had my first drink when I was fourteen?" I asked, turning to Nathan.

"Yeah."

"Well, it was at a kegger. I went because all the *cool* high school kids would be there, and I wanted to make some new friends before freshman year. I went, I drank, and I tried to have fun. And I did. The hangover was hell, though, and I

171

was sure I'd get grounded for drinking, but Mom didn't even notice. I mean, she ate breakfast with me the next morning and everything. She probably heard me puking in the toilet. But she didn't say a word.

"Since she didn't care, I thought I might as well keep going to parties. I went to a few. I met some new people. We weren't friends or anything. I didn't have friends, because my middle school best friend, Nola, had stopped hanging out with me. Some girls told her I'd give her a bad reputation or something. But these new people seemed cool. They gave me liquor, and I liked it. I liked being giggly and happy, because I didn't feel like that very often. Not since the divorce."

Nathan was quiet. I turned my head to stare out the window again, watching a few more fireworks explode in the sky. I'd never told anyone this part of the story before. No one had asked until now.

"I got really, really smashed one night at the end of freshman year. I mean, the drunkest I'd ever been in my life. I passed out at this party and ... Well, I don't really remember what happened. But I lost my virginity to a guy I didn't even know. A senior, I think. I felt somehow ... I don't know. Bonded to him? So I gave him my number. I think part of me assumed we were, like, dating or something stupid like that. Of course I don't have to tell you that he never called. I never saw him again. And I was so humiliated and ashamed."

I shifted uncomfortably, feeling Nathan's eyes on me.

"I expected Mom to say something. To scold me for the way I was acting, or at least give me the stupid safe-sex talk.

God, I came home drunk *all the time*. Sometimes I didn't come home at all. But after that I just... I expected her to see how upset I was and to ask what had happened. Maybe she couldn't tell I was depressed because she could never admit *she* was depressed, too. I don't know. But she never said a word. I mean, she has to know what I'm doing.... She and Dad both have to. Dad *has* to know, and he hasn't said *anything*."

"So you *do* want attention." It wasn't an accusation. Not harsh. Just a statement.

"Or I did. You've seen Facebook. I'm getting plenty of it now," I said.

"Yeah, but not from the right people."

I saw Nathan's fingers move on the table, spreading from a loose fist until all his fingertips touched the stained plastic. Some people would have taken my hand by now. It just went to show how well he knew me. He knew I wasn't the type to ask for comfort, so he wouldn't touch me. Wouldn't console me.

I cleared my throat. "Anyway. After that, after the first guy, I just kept partying. Maybe it only made me happy for a few hours, but at least I was happy. I tried to be more careful about how drunk I got. I've fucked up a few times, gotten trashed enough to agree to have sex, but only a few times."

I replayed the memories of those boys. Greedy hands clutching at me, pulling me, pushing me. Theirs to use for a night. I guess I was using them, too. None of them had tried to force me, but now, in my head, they all looked like Theo.

"Whitley, you don't think I... I mean, I didn't..."

"Take advantage of me? No. If anything, I probably took advantage of you. If my very fuzzy memory is correct." I smiled a little. "Sorry."

"Still," he said. "We probably shouldn't have..."

"Believe me, Nathan, if I'd known your mom was marrying my father, I wouldn't have slept with you. And I'll probably wish I hadn't told you this tomorrow, when I'm sober, but I had fun that night, thanks to you. So I don't completely regret it."

He gave me a small smile. "Do you want to know a secret?"

"I'm not promising I'll keep it," I warned, taking another sip of coffee. "As I just demonstrated, I spill my guts after I've had too much to drink."

He laughed and shook his head. "That's okay. I think I could survive, even if you did tell the world."

"You sure about that?"

"Yes, I'm sure." He leaned back in his seat, folding his arms behind his head with a sigh. "So, the truth is, I had a very, very similar experience to yours."

"Really? How's that?"

"Well, you may not realize this, but I was a big partier in high school. It's actually kind of weird we didn't run into each other a few times."

I narrowed my eyes at him. "Really? I guess I just figured that graduation party was a fluke, based on the way you've been acting."

"Hardly," he said. "That's how I know so much. Like the

mints and the coffee, and Mom's sleeping schedule. It's also how Mom knows so much about the warning signs of drinking, how she figured out what happened to Bailey. I put her through hell for, like, three years. Ever since Dad died."

"What?"

Nathan shrugged. "After Dad's heart attack sophomore year, I got really...well, angry. Mom and Bailey had each other, but I didn't have anyone. I felt like Dad had left me. Sounds dumb and selfish, I know, but that's how it felt then. Some of the guys on the basketball team asked me to come party with them. They gave me pot and beer, and before long, I wasn't angry anymore. I didn't feel anything. Then it just became a habit."

"I'm kind of shocked," I admitted. "You act like my partying is so disgusting. I just thought...I don't know what I thought."

"Sorry," he said. "I probably should have explained sooner, but I didn't really want to think about it. I'm embarrassed now, remembering some of the stupid shit I did. God knows if Mom will ever completely trust me again."

"Nathan, I'm still confused."

"Graduation night was my last party," he said. "Or at least my last drink. After that night, I decided I was done with all of it."

"Why? What changed?"

A sly grin crept across Nathan's face. "I got really, really wasted graduation night, and when I woke up, some sassy, sexy vixen had stolen my virginity."

My jaw must have hit that sticky table.

175

"I thought we'd had a great night, but when I tried to get her number, she promised she'd never see me again," he continued. "It kind of broke my heart. Call me a romantic, but I'd never expected my first time to be so...impersonal."

"You've got to be shitting me," I groaned, burying my face in my hands. "Oh my God. *Oh my God.* I was your first? Like, I took your virginity?"

"Yep."

"But...you were really good."

He blushed. "I bet you say that to all the boys."

"No, I'm serious. You were sweet, like...gentle. The other guys I've been with just..."

"Used you?"

"Yeah. I mean, I guess it goes both ways, but...you were so different."

"I liked you. I wanted to make you happy. I didn't know what the hell I was doing, but thanks for saying I was good."

"I just..." My brain was moving too slowly. My words faltered. "You...you weren't a virgin. There's no way."

"I was."

"But you're eighteen," I argued. "And hot. And a boy. You can't tell me there weren't opportunities."

"There were. I just didn't take them," he said. "I saw so many of my teammates hook up with a different girl every weekend. Sure, it sounds great, but I just wasn't into it. I didn't want to be that kind of guy. I was waiting for something special — maybe not love, and definitely not marriage,

176

but someone I liked a lot, someone I could see myself with for a while."

I felt the weight of his words sink into my stomach. He'd wanted something special, someone special. Instead he'd gotten me.

"That's why I quit drinking," he said. "After you left, I realized what I'd become, and I didn't like it. So I decided to change things. Start fresh."

"Fuck. Nathan, I'm so sorry. I didn't know."

"It's okay." He shrugged. This time, he did reach across the table to take my hand. "If it hadn't been for you, I'd still be out there getting hammered every weekend. Still driving my mother crazy. I guess I just needed someone or something to shake me up. You taught me a lesson, Whit. And sometimes I hate you for it, but... but I'm trying not to."

"You can hate me if you want to. I'd hate me."

"But I don't want to," he said. "You're part of my family — or you will be soon — and I want it to work. I've put Mom and Bailey through enough, and I want them to be happy now. That's why I try so hard to keep it bottled up, how seeing you makes me feel, but sometimes I just... I'm sorry. For some of the things I've said."

"You were right, though. About me being a whore. If I hadn't acted like such a... If I'd been different, Theo wouldn't have —"

"Stop it," he said. "I don't care how you acted. What happened tonight wasn't your fault."

"You weren't there."

"It doesn't matter. It wasn't your fault, Whitley. And you're *not* a whore."

I didn't say anything. I just stared at Nathan's hand on mine for a long moment. I'd done to him essentially the same thing that senior boy had done to me when I was fifteen. I'd used him and abandoned him and taken something from him. But instead of regressing like I had, falling into the habits and giving up on people and happiness and anything good, Nathan had worked to turn himself around, to change everything, no matter what people thought.

If he were a drug addict, I would have been his rock bottom.

"Thank you," I said.

"For what?"

"For trying not to hate me."

19

Sylvia knocked on the guest room door the next morning.
For once, she didn't wake me up. I hadn't been able to sleep
much that night, between the coffee and the terrifying memories of Theo. And staying up all night had only made the
hangover worse. This one was on par with the one I'd had the
morning after graduation.

"We need to have a talk," Sylvia said as soon as I pulled
open the door.

"Okay," I said, letting her inside.

I wasn't wearing skimpy pajamas this time. After what
had happened last night, I'd felt the need to be fully covered.
I was wearing baggy sweats and an ancient T-shirt, and it
still didn't feel like enough.

"I heard Nathan leave last night," she said, folding her

arms over her chest. "To pick you up at three AM. I thought you were staying over at Harrison's."

"I was supposed to."

I eased myself back onto the bed. Pain shot through my head, and I winced.

"Change of plans?"

"You could say that."

"Whitley," Sylvia groaned, running her hands through her hair. "Look, I don't want to be the wicked stepmother. I know what it's like to have a stepmom you hate — my stepmother treated my sister and me like we were juvenile delinquents. I don't want to be like that, but now you've clearly got a hangover, and you had Nathan out early in the morning —"

"I'm sorry," I said.

"I just can't go through this again," she went on. At first I didn't know what she meant, but then I remembered Nathan's confession. He'd said he made her crazy for years. "I don't want you to hate me, but I can't do this. I can't let my daughter be around this kind of behavior."

"I know. Like I said, I'm sorry. It won't happen again, okay?"

"My question is why you had Nathan bring you home," she said. "You were loud in the hallway this morning. If you were going to get drunk, why didn't you stay at Harrison's? You knew I'd be upset if I noticed."

My body tensed, feeling Theo's ghost fingers on my skin when she asked. I let out a breath, wrapping my arms around

180

myself. "I don't want to talk about it," I told her. "Are you going to punish me?"

She frowned. "Whitley, did something happen last night at Harrison's?"

"I don't want to talk about it, okay?" I knew my voice had risen a little too high, that my words were cracking a little too much. But I couldn't tell her. Couldn't admit what had happened with Theo. I was too angry with myself, too sure it was my fault. For drinking too much, for following him, for letting everyone think I was a slut, even if I hadn't done as much as people wanted to believe. I'd set myself up for what happened last night.

"Okay," she said. "If you change your mind ... Well, anyway, there's something else I want to talk to you about. Nathan showed me the Facebook page last night while you were out."

"God," I groaned, burying my face in my hands. "It's not ... The stuff they're saying on there — I didn't do most of it. I mean, I'm not sleeping with all those —"

"I believe you," she said. "I'm not here to call you out on it. I'm just making sure you're okay."

"Yeah. Sure, I'm fine."

"I don't know exactly what's going on with you right now," she said. "Or with that web page. But if this ... Do you think this is cyber-bullying?"

I rolled my eyes. "Christ, no. It's just stupid rumors." *Cyber-bullying.* The word felt so dramatic, like the kind of thing you might see on *Oprah* or *Dateline* or something. I wasn't one of those crying girls who'd been tortured by my classmates. I didn't even know these people.

"Are you sure?" She was dead serious about this. "Whitley, if this is getting to you, I need you to tell me. There's legal action we can take. Cyber-bullying can be very damaging."

Damaging. I wondered if Theo would have touched me if he hadn't seen that page, those pictures. I hugged myself tighter.

"It's nothing. I mean, I don't even use Facebook, so what do I care? Just leave it alone, okay? My dad's a local celebrity. People are always going to talk, right?"

She sighed. "Okay — if you're sure. But if this gets worse, if you feel like it turns into bullying at any time —"

"Yeah. I'll tell you."

"Okay." She started to stand up.

"Um, Sylvia?" I hesitated. "Has Dad said anything about it? The Facebook page?"

"I'm not even sure if he knows," she said. "Maybe it was wrong of me, but I didn't show him. I didn't know if you'd want him to see."

When the photos first came out, I hadn't wanted him to see them. But he had to have. I tried to tell myself that he'd untagged himself only yesterday, that he didn't check Facebook often, that if Sylvia cared enough to talk to me, surely he'd be up here in a few hours, too.

So I waited. After Sylvia left, repeatedly telling me that I could come to her if I needed to, I sat in my room and waited for Dad to come. I watched from the window as his car

182

pulled into the driveway after work, heard the front door shut when he came in. I thought he'd come up soon.

Trace called me that afternoon while I was still upstairs, hoping Dad would come.

"Have you talked to Mom lately?"

"No."

"You should call her," he said.

"Why?"

"Because she's your mother," he said, exasperated. "But also because she called me the other day and told me how much she misses you right now."

"She misses having someone to bitch to." I snorted. "Not me."

Trace sighed. "You're too hard on her. I mean...Okay, I don't live with her. I know that. I know she fucked up a lot. But she loves you, and it just kills me to see you putting Dad up on a pedestal when he's just as bad as she is."

"He is not," I argued. "At least Dad's fun to be around." *Not that he's around often anymore.*

"He uses you as a drinking buddy, Whitley," Trace said. "You grill burgers with him, and you drink together and hang out on the beach and drink together and, oh yeah, drink together. Whatever; I'm fine with a parent allowing his kid to drink at home, but the way you talk about your summers together, it sounds like he's more of your brother than your dad."

"Well, Trace, you've been gone for a long time. Maybe I need someone to act like my brother."

There was a long pause.

"Sorry," I said. "That was me being defensive. I'm kind of hungover and bitchy."

"I can tell."

"Look, no matter how Dad screws up, it's still better than Mom's bullshit. At least he didn't tear the family apart."

"Yes, he did."

"No, he didn't," I said. "Mom's the one who left him. Mom's the one who moved to another state. It's her fault, Trace."

I heard him let out a long breath. "I shouldn't tell you this," he said, "but you're eighteen years old, and that's old enough to know, and, God, I'm just sick of hearing the way you worship him. Whitley, Mom left because Dad cheated."

"He...what?"

"A few times," Trace said. "You were too young to know, but I figured it out. Mom asked me not to tell you then, but... Look, I know she bitches about Dad a lot and has told you things she shouldn't have, but she didn't want you to hate him, even if she does — even if he deserves it."

I didn't say anything. I just sat there, stunned.

"Mom left, but she wanted to reconcile," he continued. "Dad said no, that he'd rather be single for a while, anyway. She got pissed and moved far away. Which was wrong, I know, but... This was Dad's fault, Whitley."

Still, I couldn't say a word.

"Sorry," he said. "I know I shouldn't have told you that. Don't tell Mom. She never wanted you to find out. She'd kill me."

"I...I have to go."

"Whitley?"

"I'll call you later, okay?"

I hung up the phone before he could answer. I just sat there for a long time, staring at the blank wall. I didn't know what to think or how to feel. Trace wouldn't lie to me, I knew that, but as the clock ticked the hours past and Dad still didn't come up the stairs to see me, I really wished that I didn't know the truth.

20

I didn't leave the guest room until two o'clock the next afternoon, when I finally decided waiting on Dad wasn't doing any good — and I was hungry. When I came downstairs, I found Nathan sitting at the dining room table, hair still wet from the shower, working on his laptop. My stomach tightened.

"Are there more pictures?" I asked him from the doorway.

He looked up at me. "What?"

"On the Facebook page — are there pictures from Harrison's party?"

He sighed. "A few, but nothing too bad."

"But I bet the comments —"

"Whitley," he said, cutting me off. "Don't. Don't think about them, okay? *Fuck* those people and whatever they have to say."

"You agreed with them," I reminded him. "A few days ago, you called me a whore, too."

He looked down, staring at his lap for a moment. "Well," he said at last, "I was an asshole."

"No, you weren't." I walked over to the table and sat beside him. "You were worried about your little sister. I get that now. After last night...Christ, I'd hate myself if something like that happened to her. I hate myself as it is for what little did happen to her that night. Maybe I'm not as slutty as those comments make me out to be, but..."

"Don't get me wrong," he said. "I'm still pissed at you for not watching her that night. You screwed up. But that doesn't give these idiots the right to say the shit they're saying. I mean, seriously? How lonely and pathetic do you have to be to waste time gossiping about some girl you probably haven't met? That's pretty lame."

I smiled a little. "I guess."

"It's the truth." He paused. "So, are you okay? After what happened the other night? Harrison filled me in, but do you want to...?"

"I want to forget it ever happened," I said. "I know I won't, but I just need to think about something else for a while."

He nodded and cleared his throat, leaning back a little and clicking a few buttons on his laptop. "So, I'm looking at UK's course catalog online — checking out some classes I might want to take."

"I should do that soon," I said. "And pick a major."

"You don't have one yet?" he asked, surprised.

I shook my head. "Nope. What about you?"

"Yeah. I'm going into computer science — hoping to focus in web development."

"Oh...that's cool."

He looked at me, one eyebrow raised. "You're not going to make fun of me? Call me a nerd or anything?"

"No. Why?"

"I don't know. It just seems like something you'd do."

I laughed and stood up, walking into the kitchen. "Yeah, well, I probably would normally." I opened the fridge and pulled out an apple. "But I've decided to try this new thing and be nice to you."

He grinned at me when I sat down next to him again. "Is this because you feel guilty after what I told you at the diner?"

"Mostly," I said, chewing on my apple.

"Wow. Pity kindness. I'm flattered."

Nathan nudged my arm playfully, but the truth was that I really did feel guilty. I knew what it was like to give up something that intimate and have the person completely abandon you. I knew how shameful and hurtful it could be.

"Can I ask you something?"

He nodded. "Sure."

I took another bite of my apple and swallowed before asking, "Why did you sleep with me graduation night?"

"Because I was *really* drunk."

"Gee. Thanks."

He chuckled, scratching his head for a moment. "I told

you I was waiting for someone special, someone I really liked, right? Well, believe it or not, you're incredibly charming when you're drunk."

"Only on tequila," I said. "I learned the other night that vodka makes me a little bit of a bitch."

"Well, you were charming that night," he said. "You were friendly and funny and . . . and gorgeous."

I blushed.

"Then, when we were talking about that Van Morrison song and you told me all the songs about blue eyes . . . I don't know." He looked at me, our eyes meeting as he spoke. "I loved that you knew the old songs and that, even hammered, you could put me in my place. A lot of girls act ditzy when they're drunk, and I guess some guys think that's cute, but I don't. And you weren't like that — you seemed . . . real. We laughed a lot that night. And when you led me back to the bedroom and I knew what you wanted to do, I just remember thinking, *If this girl isn't perfect for me, no one is.* So, I guess the short answer is, I liked you. A lot."

We were still staring at each other, his brown eyes steady on mine. Suddenly, I was aware of just how close we were sitting. Our arms were almost brushing. My knee was just inches from his. I opened my mouth to say something — I had no idea what.

"Hey, kids."

I jumped and turned to look as Dad walked through the dining room. When I glanced at Nathan, I thought I saw him blushing a little. But he was back to work on his laptop, as if we hadn't been talking at all.

"Hi, Dad," I said.

"How are you this afternoon, munchkin?" he asked as he headed through the kitchen archway.

"I'm...okay. I guess." I stood up and followed him, leaving Nathan at the dining room table.

Dad moved to the counter and started sorting through a stack of mail piled there. I watched him for a moment. I hadn't seen him in days, since before he'd ditched me for Nathan and Trace had told me the truth about the divorce. It felt a little like looking at a different person. Not only had Dad changed since getting engaged to Sylvia, but he hadn't even been the man I thought he was to begin with.

He was the one responsible for our family falling apart. He'd cheated on Mom. He hadn't wanted to be with us anymore.

But he was still my dad...right? He was still the man who'd taught me how to play poker with pennies, the man who'd bought me my first Joan Jett CD, the man who'd made me watch *Animal House* and *Fast Times at Ridgemont High* and all those other R-rated classics Mom hated. He was still in there somewhere, wasn't he?

"What's up, munchkin?" he asked.

I realized I'd been standing behind him, just staring, for too long. "I, um...I was wondering if I'm grounded?"

"No," he said. "I don't think so."

"Oh," I said. "Well, Sylvia didn't tell me either way, so I thought I'd ask."

"Right," he said, still flipping through the mail, not even glancing my way. "I think we can let it slide this time." He picked up an envelope and tucked it under his arm. "I'm off to get some work done. Have a phone call with the station manager in half an hour. He wants me to pitch in the network softball game against 97.5 — that Top 40 radio network. Might be fun. Anyway." He turned and kissed me on the top of my head. "See you at dinner."

He walked out of the kitchen, clapping Nathan on the shoulder as he passed through the dining room.

"Hey, Greg."

"Working hard, Nate?"

"Of course not."

Dad laughed. "Oh, to be eighteen again."

I stood in the kitchen for a long moment after he'd gone. I'd been waiting for him to come upstairs, waiting for him to talk to me about those pictures. Sylvia had, but Dad had just ignored them.

All summer I'd thought Dad's distance from me was a new thing, but maybe it wasn't. Maybe I'd just been making excuses for him. For why he never called, why he could only see me once a year.

Trace said Dad hadn't reconciled the marriage because he wanted to be single, because he didn't want a family. I remembered being fourteen, begging him to let me live with him. Mom was always either yelling or sleeping, and I didn't have friends. I was miserable and I needed him. It dawned on me just then that he hadn't said no because he cared for Mom. He'd said no because he didn't want me.

A few minutes later, when I was back in the guest room, I pulled out the bottle of Margaritaville. I stared at it for a long moment, thinking of finishing off the last little bit. It would be nice to get buzzed right now. It would make me laugh and smile. Like Nathan said, I was fun when I was drunk.

I thought of Bailey, of how I hadn't protected her. I thought of Nathan's hand reaching across the table at the diner, his fingers covering mine. I cared about Bailey and Nathan cared about me. This wouldn't make things with Dad any better. This wouldn't make me forget. It would just hurt them. And I didn't want to hurt them. Not more than I already had.

I carried the bottle into the bathroom, checking to make sure the hallway was clear first. I poured out the last few drops of tequila, watching as the only thing that had made me happy over the past few years trickled down the drain. Going, going...gone.

21

I didn't leave the house at all over the next week. I spent most
of my time locked in the guest room or watching Bailey practice her cheers. Occasionally, Harrison would come over and
hang out, but we never went to the Nest or to parties or anything after the Fourth of July.

But that didn't stop people from posting on the Facebook
page.

Nathan usually wouldn't let me look on his computer, but
sometimes I'd sneak into his room when he had run downstairs. He had a bad habit of leaving his computer on, and he
was always logged on to Facebook.

Pictures from Harrison's party; speculations of what I'd
do next; insults about my clothes, my hair, the size of my ass.
Everything. And Dad was tagged in so much of it. Tagged

one day, untagged the next. And still not a word to me. Not that I expected it anymore.

Every time I saw him in the house, every time he asked me to pass the rolls at dinner, every time he called during a break at work to ask Nathan to pick something up at the grocery store and I answered the phone — I wanted to scream every time. To throw things. To ask him why he loved them more than me. But I held it in. I didn't want to know the answer to that question.

He must have been counting down the days until I left, until it could just be him and his perfect family and he could go back to pretending I didn't exist.

As angry as I was, part of me didn't blame him.

I stood in the living room and watched them through the screen door. Sherri was visiting for the afternoon. She and Sylvia sat in lawn chairs, drinking lemonade while Dad and Nathan played one-on-one basketball in the driveway. Bailey was doing back handsprings in the grass, as if she were a cheerleader at a big game.

Sherri and Sylvia clapped and laughed as Nathan threw the ball into the hoop above the garage, sinking it perfectly. Dad's lips were moving quickly, clearly arguing that, somehow, that shot hadn't been fair.

I felt like I was watching a home movie. A good one. It was like you could *see* the joy and the love. They were palpable.

Nathan saw me standing in the doorway. He raised a hand and waved, gesturing for me to join them.

But I shook my head.

I ran upstairs before anyone else could turn around and see me.

Later, after dinner, Nathan followed me into the guest room. "Why didn't you come outside earlier?"

I sighed and sat down on my bed. "I had a stomachache."

He frowned at me. "Really, Whit?"

"Whitley," I corrected automatically.

"I don't believe you," he said. "About the stomachache."

"I just didn't want to, okay?"

That wasn't entirely a lie.

The truth was that I hadn't wanted to ruin it. Dad and the Caulfields were perfect together. They were a family. A beautiful family. More of a family than Mom, Dad, Trace, and I had been, even before the divorce. Nathan and Bailey had both tried to make me feel welcome, but I still didn't belong. I was the puzzle piece that didn't fit.

Nathan watched me for a long moment. Then he sat down on the bed next to me, one arm curving around my shoulders. I couldn't tell if the gesture was meant to be platonic or romantic. I couldn't tell which I wanted it to be.

"Well, I hate for you to miss out on all the fun," he said. "So why don't you join Bailey and me for movies tonight?"

"Nathan..."

"I want you to," he said firmly. "And so will she."

I forced a smile. "Okay. But I'm not watching *Bring It On* again."

"Damn. I am just so heartbroken by that," he joked.

I tried to call Trace after Nathan had gone, but I only got his voice mail.

Trace had a family now, too. A gorgeous wife and daughter. A family of his own. One I wasn't part of.

And no matter whose fault it was, Mom and I hadn't been a family in a long time.

I didn't know who I was without the parties or drinking or boys that had been my life for the past four years. I had nothing. No one. I didn't know where I belonged anymore.

"You have one unheard message.... First unheard message."

"Whitley, it's your mom. I haven't heard from you in a while, and I just wanted to check in. Trace says he's talked to you a few times, but I haven't, so...give me a call? I miss you, honey. I hope you're having fun.... But listen, if anything's going on with your father, you can let me know and —"

"Message deleted."

"Physics?"

"No. No science."

"Politics?"

"No."

"Psychology?"

"I'm too screwed up to be a psychologist."

"Oh, what about Russian? Russian could be cool."

I looked at Harrison over the top of my sunglasses. We were lying in lawn chairs by the pool. The UK course catalog was in Harrison's lap, and he'd flipped to the list of majors.

"*Russian*? Really, Harrison?"

"I took Russian in high school," Nathan said, climbing out of the pool. He'd decided to swim laps that afternoon instead of going to the gym.

"Did you?" Harrison asked, grinning at him.

"Yeah." Nathan grabbed his towel from the little patio table and began dabbing at his face. "But the only thing I remember is, *Mozhno li kopirovat vashi domashnie zadaneeye?*"

"Let me guess," I said. "You just asked me where the bathroom is, right?"

"No." He scoffed, flicking his wet towel at me. "I was beyond that basic stuff. I took two years of it. Give me some credit."

"Then what does it mean?" I asked.

"It means, 'Can I copy your homework?'"

Harrison laughed, as if this were the funniest thing in the world. I just smiled and shook my head. "Did you say that a lot?" I asked Nathan.

"Every morning before class started." He grinned at me before slinging the towel over his shoulder. "All right. I'm heading inside. You two have a good time."

"Have a nice night, Nathan!" Harrison called out. We both watched him go, and when the screen door closed, Harrison added quietly, "Now, I would major in *that*."

"Shut up."

"I'm just saying." He looked down at the catalog again. "We're almost at the end of the list, Whitley. Unless you want to look in the Engineering school — but I'm assuming you don't."

"Definitely not."

"You like music," he said. "Ever thought of majoring in it?"

I cringed. Theo was a music major. That night, I'd even said I might consider it. Now I knew I never would.

"I don't play anything," I told Harrison. "Besides, I don't think you study Nirvana or Blondie or the Ramones in college. I'd get bored with all the classical shit."

"Fashion?"

"UK doesn't have a fashion school."

"Come out to L.A. with me, then," he said. "Be my room-mate, and I'll dress you every day. You know you want to."

That actually didn't sound too bad. Trace was in Los Angeles. And the whole reason I'd picked UK was because it was Dad's alma mater. I always thought I wanted to be like him. Not so much anymore.

"I can't. UK's already been paid."

Harrison sighed. "Then I don't know what to tell you. Any ideas what you want to do after college? What makes you happy?"

That was the million-dollar question. Because I honestly had no idea. Drinking had made me happy, but there wasn't a major in alcoholism, to the best of my knowledge.

When I didn't answer, Harrison changed the subject. "Hey, I'm going out with Wesley and Bianca tonight. Want to join us so I don't have to be a third wheel?"

I shook my head.

"Why not?"

"I don't think his girlfriend likes me too much," I said.

"Bianca? Why do you think that?"

"Because the first time she met me I was trying to seduce her boyfriend. Pretty sure that pissed her off a little."

Harrison laughed. "Well, you wouldn't be the first. But she'll get over it. Come out with us. Dinner, a movie, maybe a little happy hour at my place afterward? No extra guests this time. Just the four of us."

"No, I...I think I'd rather stay in."

"Whitley," he said, frowning. "You've stayed in every night since the party at my place. Have you even left the house? Been to the grocery store? Anything?"

I didn't answer.

"What happened with Theo isn't going to happen again," he said quietly. "I promise. I'm not going to let anyone hurt you."

"It's not that...not *just* that. Look, I don't want to go out, okay? I'm sorry."

He studied me for a while longer, his green eyes narrowing, dark eyebrows pulled together just a little. Then, finally, he nodded. "Fine. Okay, let's see what other majors are listed here.... Oh, sociology?"

"No."

22

Sylvia had to work the day Gwyneth's Bridal Boutique called to say I needed to come in and try on my bridesmaid dress. Bailey's had been done for a while; now it was my turn. It was the first time I'd left the house in two weeks. You'd think I would have been getting cabin fever, but this was a trip I wasn't looking forward to. Especially once I found out Harrison wasn't working that day — which meant I'd have to deal with Sexy Lexie. If my dress wasn't enough to make me self-conscious, having Lexie around certainly did the trick.

"Come out, Whit."

"No."

"Whit."

"No."

Like I said, Sylvia was at work, and Dad had some sort

of meeting at the station that afternoon, so Nathan drove me to the fitting.

"I won't laugh," he assured me from outside the dressing room. "I promise."

"I don't believe you."

"I really don't have all day," I heard Lexie say with exasperation. "There are two others coming in for fittings today."

I gritted my teeth, trying to convince myself that my annoyance with her was due to her pushiness and was completely unrelated to the way she'd been flirting with Nathan since the moment we walked into the store. No, I didn't like her because she was being bossy — that was the only reason.

I took a deep breath and ran my hands over the dress, smoothing a few tiny wrinkles in the front. There was no mirror behind the curtain, so I could only guess how it looked. The sleeves had already been cut and the hem shortened to knee-length, but nothing could be done to fix the color. I could not *believe* I would be forced to wear this thing in front of a large crowd in, like, a month and a half.

Maybe I just wouldn't show up to the wedding. It wasn't like I'd be missed.

"Whit," Nathan called again teasingly. "You heard the girl. We don't have all day. Come out."

"Fine!" I shouted. "Goddamn it."

I shoved open the curtain and stepped into the room where Nathan and Lexie waited. Both their gazes fell upon me. I could feel them examining every inch of the dress, of my frame. I closed my eyes so I couldn't see their reactions.

201

"Let's see," Lexie said, stepping up behind me. Her hands moved down the length of the dress, tugging at the straps and pulling at the hem. "Not a bad fit. I think we can take it in just a little at the waist. Otherwise, you're good."

I opened my eyes as she stepped away from me.

"Am I done?"

"Mm-hmm," Lexie said, jotting something down on her tiny little notepad. "We'll make the alteration and the dress will be done in plenty of time. I'll go save this in your file now."

"Great," I muttered.

Lexie strutted back into the main part of the shop, leaving Nathan and me alone in the back room. I glanced at him, expecting to find his eyes on her back, watching her perfect little figure move away. Instead, he was staring at me.

"What?" I asked.

"You look —"

"Like a giant stick of bubble gum. Yeah, I know."

"No," he said. "That's not what I was going to say."

"Really? What then?"

"I was going to say you look beautiful."

I snorted, but I could feel my cheeks heating up. "Whatever. In this dress? I doubt it."

"Seriously," he said. "Come look."

He stepped forward and grabbed my hand, pulling me across the room, toward the full-length mirror that hung on the wall. I rolled my eyes as he positioned me in front of it, his hands on my shoulders.

Surprisingly, the dress didn't look half bad. The shade of pink was still kind of obnoxious, but I managed to pull it off. The little flowers around my torso were actually kind of cute, and the dress suited my figure — the hourglass skirt and sweetheart neckline made me look taller, more refined. Definitely not as hideous as I'd thought.

"See," Nathan said. The mirror reflected his grin, his face bobbing just over my head. "Beautiful."

"Yeah," I agreed. My gaze fell on Nathan's hands, still curved over my shoulders, then traveled back up to his smiling face. His brown eyes were light and warm. Staring at me as I stared at him. "Beautiful."

Once I'd changed, Nathan and I headed back toward the doors of the shop. Lexie was waiting for us there. She didn't even look at me as we approached.

"Nathan," she said, stepping out from behind the register. "Listen, I know you said you're starting college at the end of the summer, right? Well, if you ever want to get together, to ask me about college…or, you know, just hang out…" She slipped a piece of paper into his hand. "Give me a call."

"Whit, wait up," Nathan said, since I was already halfway out the door. "Thanks, Lexie." Then he jogged over to me, pushing the door open the rest of the way so I could walk out ahead of him. "In a hurry?" he asked.

"No."

"Sure seems like it," he said. "Are you hungry? We can stop somewhere if you want. It's past lunchtime."

"Yeah," I said. "I guess I could go for a bite to eat."

"Cool. Hold on just a second." He left me standing on the sidewalk while he walked over to the closest Dumpster. I watched as he tossed Lexie's number into the trash. Then he was next to me again, leading the way to the car. "Red Lobster sound good to you? My aunt gave me a gift card for graduation."

I smiled, half at him and half to myself. "That sounds great."

23

"You totally have a thing for him."

I turned to face Harrison. "What are you talking about?"

It was a hot afternoon in late July. Harrison was off work, and we were swimming in Dad and Sylvia's pool. Nathan had just climbed out of the water and walked inside, saying something about a game on ESPN Classic.

"You watched him walk away like you were fantasizing about his hot little ass. You *like* him."

"How would you know?" I demanded, splashing water in Harrison's face. "You were watching him, too."

"*Too!*" he cried. "I got you! Ha. You just admitted you were watching him. You love him. You so love him."

"I do not," I said. "That's just weird, okay? He's going to be my stepbrother."

"I know. It's all sexy and forbidden — like in *Cruel Intentions.*"

"Doesn't someone die at the end of that movie?" I asked. "Not that it matters. I don't like him that way. We're just... I don't know. Lately we've hung out more. He's not so bad, really. So, I guess we're friends now."

"Friends with benefits," Harrison teased.

I tried not to blush or anything dumb like that. Harrison didn't know about my past with Nathan. I'd never told him about the graduation party or the aloe incident or the almost-hookup in the guest room. I hadn't breathed a word, and I wasn't planning to. Because that was all behind me. Harrison could believe what he wanted, but I was done chasing boys. Nathan and I were friends. Just friends. And future stepsiblings. That was all.

"You're just dreaming," I told Harrison. "You can't have him, so you want to live vicariously through me."

"Damn straight I do."

"Christ, Harrison, you're such a loser," I joked, splashing him again.

He splashed me back, and soon a war erupted in the water around us. And the issue was dropped.

Unfortunately, Bailey wasn't so easily distracted... or convinced.

"So, what's going on with you and my brother?" she asked the next day. Her cheerleading tryouts were in a week, and we were out on the front lawn practicing again. I was no expert, but it seemed like she was doing well.

"What do you mean?"

"Something is up with you and Nathan," she insisted, sitting down on the porch beside me.

"I don't know what you're talking about," I said, handing her a bottle of water. Christ, I just couldn't catch a break about this.

"I'm not stupid." She unscrewed the cap and downed a few gulps of water, letting some of the clear liquid drip down her chin. "You're being nice to him. I thought you hated him."

"Why would you think that?"

"You guys were just so weird around each other." She handed the bottle back to me. "It was always, like, tense. You were pissed off —"

"It's still weird when you say pissed."

"Now you hang out and run errands together and smile at each other —"

"Your mom made him drive me to the bridal shop," I said. "That doesn't count as hanging out."

"But you watch movies together, too. I told you, I'm not stupid. I can see that something changed. What happened?"

Goddamn, the kid asked way too many questions.

"I don't know," I said flatly. "Why does it matter?"

"I'm just curious."

"Well, you're wasting time. You should practice."

"I have practiced."

"Practice more."

"Why are you changing the subject?" She raised a little blond eyebrow at me. "You act like you're hiding something, Whitley."

"I'm not."

"Are you sure?"

I rolled my eyes. "You're so annoying," I said, nudging her arm. "If you want me to hate your brother, I will. Would that make you happy?"

"No, I just —"

"Then practice and let it go."

She frowned at me. "Fine. But I think you're hiding something."

Before I could argue, she skipped across the yard and did two cartwheels in a row. "Go, go, Panthers!" she yelled, finishing with a backflip and a toe touch.

The kid was lucky I couldn't get angry with her; even when she was being irritating, I still kind of adored her.

It seemed like the only one not questioning my relationship with Nathan was, well, Nathan. He had no issue with our sudden friendship. He invited me to go places with him, obviously aware that my social life was lacking due to my self-imposed isolation.

The next Friday night, while Bailey went to sleep over at Sherri's, Nathan asked me to have a *Back to the Future* movie marathon with him. He claimed that I had to join him because it was a travesty that I'd yet to see these movies —

208

which, I might add, came out way before I was born. I didn't put up much of a fight, though. It was the third Friday night in a row that I'd stayed in, and a little company, even if it was just Nathan, was preferable to lying on the guest bed, listening to my iPod for hours on end.

He tapped on the guest room door around nine. "Are you ready for the epicness you are about to witness?" he asked.

"When you say *epic*, are you describing the movies or your shocking level of nerdiness?"

"Hey," he said, folding his arms over his chest, only barely obscuring the image of a hand making the Vulcan salute on his T-shirt. "I thought you were giving this whole being-nice thing a try."

"I am," I told him. "But come on. You want to major in computer science, you're practically swooning over some ancient movie about a time-traveling car, and you have a freaking Darth Vader bobblehead in your room. I thought jocks beat up geeks, not aspired to be them."

"What can I say? I'm a complicated guy."

"If that's what you want to believe..."

I followed Nathan into the hallway, but instead of heading downstairs, he turned toward his bedroom. When he noticed me staring, he said, "Mom and Greg are watching something in the living room. I figured we could just watch the movies on my laptop — is that cool?"

I shrugged. "Fine by me."

We sat side by side on his bed, our bodies turned toward

the desk, where his laptop played the film on its small monitor. I had to admit, *Back to the Future* wasn't so bad. I even enjoyed parts of it.

"But Marty McFly is, like, the worst name *ever*."

"Says the girl whose parents couldn't spell Whit*ney*. Can you really judge?"

I jammed my elbow into his ribs. "Whitley is a real name, thank you. Christ — and Bailey thinks I'm the one who's mean to *you*?"

He winked. "The tables have turned, it appears."

"And payback is a bitch."

"Just like you."

I stuck my tongue out at him.

"You're so mature," he said. "I'm just blown away by your maturity."

"Shut up and watch your movie."

By the time Nathan wanted to start the sequel, I was feeling tired. Since I'd had nowhere to go and nothing to do for weeks, I'd gotten into the habit of going to bed kind of early. It was barely eleven now and I was exhausted. But Nathan insisted I had to stay up for the whole thing.

"This one is my favorite," he said. "Come on. In bed before midnight? On a weekend? Even my mother isn't that lame."

"I'm not lame," I snapped, taking the DVD case from him and hopping off the bed. I took out the disc and popped it into the laptop.

"But you are easily swayed by peer pressure," he teased.

I hit play and joined him on the bed again. "I convinced

you to give up your virginity within two hours or so of knowing you. Let's not talk about caving to peer pressure."

"Touché."

But no matter how I tried — or how many times Nathan poked me in the ribs to keep me awake — I just kept nodding off, my head bobbing up and down as I tried to hold my eyes open.

I didn't realize I'd dozed off until hours later when I opened my eyes. The lights were still on in the bedroom, and the menu screen for *Back to the Future Part II* showed on the monitor. The clock on the desk told me it was just after three in the morning.

Nathan and I were lying crookedly on his bed, huddled together in a way that, even half-asleep, I knew could only be described as cuddling. My head was propped on his chest, its rise and fall a gentle lull, calling me back toward sleep. My left arm was stretched loosely across his torso. He was snoring softly, with one of his hands resting on my hip. How we'd ended up this way, I wasn't sure, but somehow, between both of us conking out, we'd managed to twine together like this.

I sat up, easing myself out of Nathan's grasp and climbing off his bed. He looked so peaceful sleeping there. I backed toward the door. It had felt good to have him next to me like that.

I'd liked it — cuddling with Nathan.

And I wasn't sure I was supposed to like it.

I hurried back to the guest room, shutting the door silently behind me so as not to wake anyone. Now *I* was questioning

211

my relationship with Nathan, too. How did I feel about this guy? Did it cross the line between stepsiblings? *Future* stepsiblings? Did I want it to?

Shit, shit, shit.

I was going to kill Harrison and Bailey for putting these ideas in my head.

Right when I'd started to like — or at least not hate — Sylvia Caulfield, she decided to go and piss me off again.

On the last Saturday in July, Dad was ordered to go pick out his wedding tux. And I, for some reason, was required to go with him.

"You know he has horrible taste. You're the only one I trust with choosing something this important," she said.

She was hoping to make it sound like a privilege or something. Yeah, right. Dad had great taste in clothes. He picked out all of his TV suits. She was just making shit up to persuade me.

"You'll be saving the whole family from a world of embarrassment."

"Why can't you go with him?" I whined.

There were a multitude of reasons why I didn't want to go shopping with my father. In particular, the overwhelming desire I had to punch him in the face every time I saw him came to mind.

I'd spent the last two months attempting to talk to my father. The summer was almost over now, and my frustration had morphed into pure anger. He'd cheated on Mom, he'd let me spend the last six years blaming her, and he hadn't cared enough to confront me about my behavior or let me live with him four years ago, when my world first started falling apart.

I didn't want to talk to him now. I didn't want anything to do with him.

"You're off today," I reminded her. "You can go."

"You two need to spend some time together." She said it so forcefully that I knew arguing would be pointless.

"Fine," I muttered, poking the waffle in front of me with the tip of my fork. Sylvia made real waffles, not the toaster ones Mom always made for us. I would have never admitted it to Sylvia, especially that morning when I was so pissed at her, but she really was an amazing cook.

"Whitley." Sylvia sighed. "Honey, you've been here since May, and you haven't even unpacked your bag."

I didn't look at her.

"I know you're not happy and that you must be frustrated," she said. "But you're only here for a few more weeks. I don't want you going off to college with regrets about your relationship with your father."

"He'd be the one with regrets," I mumbled.

I didn't think she'd heard me, but apparently she had. "That might be true, but you need to put forth a little effort, too. He loves you."

"Whatever."

"I'll take that to mean you'll go with him."

"Do I have a choice?"

213

"Not really." She smiled and took my plate of syrup. "He'll be ready and in the car by ten."

So, when I climbed into the SUV an hour and a half later, Dad was all pumped and ready to go. He grinned at me from across the cab. And for a moment, I thought maybe Sylvia was right. Maybe this time together would be good. Maybe we could work things out....

"Hey, munchkin. Nice to see you up so early."

"I was forced."

He laughed and started the engine, humming along with the country music on the radio. I frowned. At one time, we'd both hated country music. Jimmy Buffett was the only exception. But I guess that was just one more thing to show me how much my dad had changed. We didn't even hate the same things anymore.

And if I had hopes of getting to know the new Dad on this little outing, they were dashed the minute we got to the tuxedo place. It was like I wasn't there anymore. Just him and the tuxes — and there were lots of tuxes. He insisted on trying on all of them. Because nothing was good enough.

That coat was too tacky.

That bow tie was too small.

Those pants had a strange shape.

My father shopped like a woman, which made Sylvia's whole pretense of me saving him from wardrobe embarrass-ment even more laughable. *Laughable* was also a great word to describe the bonding idea. This was real quality time, with

Dad locked in a dressing room and me sitting on the bench outside, texting Harrison about how the store attendant was just his type.

But I couldn't get Sylvia's voice out of my head, and I knew that it was still my job to try. So, after three hours of shopping — during which time Dad wound up buying the first of the twenty-two tuxes he'd tried on — I swallowed my pride and made my attempt to talk to him.

I suggested we go get ice cream together, and I started the conversation.

"So," I began, swirling the plastic spoon around in my Dairy Queen Blizzard. "We, um, haven't really had a chance to talk in a while."

"I know," Dad said. "I'm sorry about that, munchkin. I've just been so busy. Between work and preparing for this wedding and just getting used to everything. Becoming part of a family can be difficult."

You were already part of one.

"Yeah," I said. "I guess it probably can be.... But the Caulfields are nice, I guess."

"I thought you'd love them."

"I wish you'd told me about them."

He sighed. "I suppose I probably should have. It just didn't seem right, you know? To tell you over the phone or in an e-mail that I was engaged."

"You could have told me when you started dating her. You could have called."

"Oh, you know, me, munchkin." He laughed. "I had no idea how serious it would be. I didn't see any need to waste your time by telling you about another girlfriend when I figured she'd be gone in a month or two."

I gritted my teeth. Whose time did he really think he'd be wasting by calling me? Mine or his?

"Then we were serious all of a sudden," he continued. "And I just thought I should give you the news in person."

"Right. Well, I like them. Nathan and Bailey are nice, and Sylvia...She's been really great support through all of this online-bullying stuff." I waited to see if he'd even admit knowing about it, or if he'd feign ignorance.

"Yeah," he said. "Well, Sylvia says you're holding up well."

Fuck that. Holding up well? He hadn't spoken to me about the pictures, hadn't acknowledged them. He'd just untagged himself and ignored them, never even asking if I was okay. Sylvia shouldn't have been the one talking to me about cyber-bullying. It should have been him — my *father*. He didn't even care.

But like an idiot, I just kept trying.

"The things they said — most of them weren't true," I told him.

"Good."

"Do...do you want to talk about it?" I asked. "I mean, I know some of it was on your Facebook page. Did you want to ask me about any of the pictures or...anything?"

"No, munchkin. I have faith that you can deal with it," he said.

I stared at him, trying to fight off the tears springing to my eyes. Even if he wasn't angry, couldn't he have given me a hug? Comforted me? I wanted to throw my ice cream at him. To scream, *Everyone in this fucking town thinks I'm a whore because of that web page! I was almost raped a few weeks ago because of some of the things it says about me! The least you could do is tell me you give a shit.*

But I didn't say anything.

"We should get back," Dad said, standing up. We'd been sitting in the booth for barely ten minutes. "Sylvia will be wondering what's taking us so long."

"Wait — I need...Can I ask you something?"

"Sure, munchkin. What's up?"

I swallowed. I couldn't believe I was going to ask him this. I was such a moron.

"A few years ago, when I asked to live with you, you said no. Was it really because of Mom? Because you didn't want her to be upset?"

"Of course."

"Really?"

"Well...why are you asking me about this?" he asked.

"Just because. Because I should know. Was there another reason you didn't want me to live with you?"

He let out a long breath and pressed three fingers to his temple. "That was a big part of the reason, yes. Because I knew your mother was very upset about the divorce and if you came to live with me, she'd be even more upset. I felt guilty, and I didn't want to make things worse."

"But this was two years after the divorce," I told him. "It was over with. She was still mad, but... What was the other reason, Dad?"

"Whitley, I don't —"

"Just tell me."

"To be honest, I was happy. I was a bachelor with a good job and a great life. I'd just gotten out of a marriage I'd been in since I was twenty-one, and I was having fun. I didn't think it was the right time."

"Right time for what?" I asked. "For me to live with you?"

He shook his head. "Having a teenage girl live with me would have complicated things."

"So...you just...didn't want me?"

I'd already figured this out, but hearing it out loud still hurt like hell.

"I wouldn't say it like that. It was more just...I know I was a bad father for feeling that way, but I thought, in the long run, life would be better for both of us if you just stayed with your mother. I was sure you were just going through a phase — wanting to live with me. You were fourteen. You'd change your mind. I shouldn't have lied to you. But it all worked out in the end, right?"

"Right," I muttered.

"Okay, let's get out of here." He stood and picked up his empty cup of ice cream. "I'm sorry, munchkin. I wish I could have told you the truth then, but I was a selfish asshole. I've changed, though."

No, I thought, watching him toss his cup in the trash can and head for the door. I stood up and followed, throwing away my unfinished Blizzard. *That's one thing about you that hasn't changed at all.*

24

Right after we got back to the house, I received a text message from Trace.

Hey sry havent called n a while. Em got a new job! How r u?

His timing was pretty uncanny. Dad was walking into the kitchen, leaving me standing in the living room, alone, without even a word. Like nothing had happened. Like I wasn't there. It was like Trace knew I needed him. Like he knew how alone I felt.

I started texting back as I walked upstairs to the guest room.

Not good. Can I call u?

He replied quickly.

No. N a meeting. On a saturday. Its boring & its a long story. I
can txt tho

Leave it to my brother to be texting under the table at
some kind of important meeting. A good sister would have
sent him another message, telling him she'd call him when
the meeting was over. He shouldn't be texting. This was his
job. All of that bullshit.

Well, I wasn't a good sister. In fact, I was pretty goddamn
selfish if you got right down to it. Yet another trait I'd gotten
from my father, I guess.

There were so many things I wanted to say. So many stories I wanted to tell Trace. Feelings I wanted him to understand. But a text message can't hold that many emotions. Or
letters.

So I typed the only words that seemed to fit:

I liked dad better b4 I knew the truth.

It wasn't easy explaining to Trace through text messages the
whole story about my talk with Dad, but I managed. And
while his attempts to comfort me were full of misspellings
and incorrect punctuation, it felt good just to have someone
listen. Or read, technically.

He told me he'd give me a call — a *real* voice-to-voice

call — in the next few days, but I wasn't going to hold him to it. Not that I thought he was lying or anything, but he had a wife now. A daughter. And at the moment, I was beginning to understand just how important it could be for a father to pay attention to his family.

Trace's family came first. I got that. Even if taking care of them meant he couldn't call me for several days, I wouldn't complain. Not anymore.

Thingsll get better. Dont 4get hes still r dad. He fucked up but he luvz u

I didn't reply to that one. Lately, everyone seemed to be telling me that Dad loved me. Everyone but Dad.

I put my cell phone on the nightstand and stretched out on the bed, squeezing my eyes shut. With all the things I'd learned, I knew that even when the summer ended, the nightmare wouldn't. I was mad at Dad for so many things, but mostly I was mad at him for letting me see he wasn't perfect.

I didn't open my eyes even when I heard the door of the guest room open.

"Hey, Whit," Nathan said. "Bailey and I are going to the movies. You want to come?"

"No," I muttered.

"You sure?" he asked. "It'll be fun."

"I'm sure."

The latch on the door clicked, and I figured Nathan had gone. But of course he hadn't. The end of the bed sank a little beneath his weight, and I sighed loudly.

"What?" I demanded, opening my eyes and finding Nathan sitting next to me.

"Did something happen today?" he asked. "With you and Greg?"

Every bone in my body told me to scream, *None of your goddamn business!* But looking up into Nathan's chocolate eyes, I just couldn't. As much as I wanted to blame the Caulfields for the way Dad had changed, I knew now that he'd been flawed for a long time. And they — Nathan, Bailey, and Sylvia — had been good to me, no matter how I treated them in return.

"Yeah." I sat up. "I tried to talk to him, but he just doesn't care. I brought up the Internet stuff, and he said he was sure I could handle it. That was all."

"I'm sorry," Nathan said.

"There was more, but... You know, I think he's always been this selfish, I just didn't want to see it." I pressed my fingertips to my eyes as the tears I'd fought off at Dairy Queen began sliding down my cheeks. "I hate this. I've spent years being an apathetic, coldhearted bitch, not caring about anyone. But he's turned me into a sniveling little girl with Daddy Issues."

He lifted his arms a bit, then hesitated. I shook my head and scooted closer to him, resting my forehead against his shoulder. He smelled like soap and spice, and his cotton

T-shirt was soft against my face. His arms were around me then, hugging me. I didn't cry long — just for a few moments. One of Nathan's hands stroked my hair gently, the way someone should always do when they comfort you. The way mothers do in movies when their little girls wake up from nightmares. The way fathers on TV do when their daughters have their hearts broken for the first time.

The way no one ever had for me.

When the tears were done, I sat up, swiping my wrist across my wet cheeks and eyes. "I'm sorry. God, I'm ridiculous."

"No, you're not."

We sat in silence for a long time, just breathing the stale air of the guest room together. After a moment, Nathan looked at me.

"Are you sure you don't want to come with Bailey and me?" he asked. "The movie's a comedy. Maybe it will cheer you up."

I shook my head. "No. I don't think so. I'm just going to stay here and..."

He stared at me, waiting.

"And do something. I don't know."

"You think you'll call Harrison?" Nathan asked. "Maybe he'll come hang out with you or something."

"Maybe." *No.* "Have fun," I told Nathan, pulling my hair over my shoulder and absently twisting the brown strands around my fingers. "I hope the movie is good."

"Okay," he said, nodding. He reached over and squeezed

my arm before standing up. "Well, we aren't leaving for half an hour, if you change your mind."

Then he was gone.

Nathan and Bailey had already gone to the movies by the time I finally left the guest room that night. I was starting to get hungry, and Sylvia hadn't called me down for dinner or anything yet. So I slumped into the kitchen and began digging through the cabinets, hoping I might find some Pop-Tarts to snack on.

I'd just located a box of strawberry ones — my favorite — when the screen door slid open and Sylvia walked in, wearing her swimsuit and laughing loudly. She stopped when she saw me, her cheeks turning instantly scarlet.

"Whitley," she said. "Hey. I thought you'd gone out with the kids."

"No," I said, unwrapping my Pop-Tart. "I decided to stay home."

"Oh, sorry," Sylvia said, putting a hand to her mouth. I could see a small key dangling from a chain around her finger. "Sweetie, if I'd known you were staying here, I would have made something for you to eat. Gosh, I'm so sorry."

"It's cool."

She walked past me and reached for the cabinet above the sink, sliding the little silver key from her finger and opening the lock.

Liquor cabinet.

Somehow, I couldn't believe she kept alcohol in the house.

Sylvia pulled down a bottle of wine. "You sure you can fend for yourself tonight?" she asked, relocking the cabinet.

"Yeah. No problem."

"Good," she said, and she turned to me with a sigh. "Sometimes I need a night off." She laughed and ran her fingers through her wet hair. "Okay. I'll see you in the morning, Whitley."

"See you."

She smiled, and I noticed the bounce in her step as she headed toward the screen door. When she walked outside, I could hear the music playing. Familiar and sweet.

. . . Some people claim that there's a woman to blame, but I know . . .

The door slid shut again, silencing the sounds of Jimmy Buffett and "Margaritaville." But I'd heard it. I could have recognized that song by two notes alone. I'd listened to it so many times during summers at the condo.

I ran to the door, still holding my Pop-Tart, and peeked out through the screen. Dad was sitting in one of the lawn chairs, wearing his swim trunks, as Sylvia twirled and danced her way over to the table. She sat down across from him and opened the bottle of wine she'd just taken from the liquor cabinet, sipping straight from the top before passing it to Dad.

He lifted the bottle to his mouth, but his lips were already moving, forming the lyrics of the song.

He was singing.

And Sylvia was laughing.

And they were drinking.

It was like a scene from a movie I'd watched over and over and over again. That was Summer Dad sitting out there. The Dad I'd missed. The Dad I'd assumed was gone. But he was here. With Sylvia.

I stepped away from the door, fists clenched.

All summer I'd looked for him. My laid-back, laughing, best friend of a dad. But he'd been here all along. Two months, and I hadn't seen him. Now, he sat just outside with his new fiancée, living his new life.

I swung my fist into the side of the fridge. Then again. I left my Pop-Tart on the table and ran back upstairs, slamming every door between there and the guest room.

I'd missed him. I'd missed him so much, and he'd been there all along. Just not with me.

25

"Please."

"No."

"Come on, Whit. Please?"

"Leave me alone, Nathan."

It was the beginning of August, about a week after the bad shopping day with Dad, and Nathan had decided to spend that Friday afternoon harassing me.

The fact was that I hadn't been in a good mood since Saturday. Seeing Dad being his old self again — without me — had hurt almost as much as Dad's admission about not wanting me to live with him four years ago. Since that night, I hadn't left the guest room much, going downstairs only for meals, and I hadn't spoken a word to Dad.

Nathan wasn't making things much better. He'd been banging on the guest-room door for the past ten minutes, bugging the shit out of me. I knew what he wanted. He'd been trying to convince me to go to the Nest with him for days. He claimed it would cheer me up. Get me out of this funk I had fallen into.

At first, I'd politely — well, kind of politely — told him I wasn't interested. I just didn't feel like it. Not tonight. Maybe another time. Try again later.

He asked every single goddamn night, always showing up with a new argument. I knew he was doing it because he cared. Because we were friends ... or *something*. But it still got annoying fast.

And he was back again, knock, knock, knocking away at the door.

Finally sick of yelling through the door at him, I yanked it open, positioning myself carefully in front of it so he couldn't get in. "No," I said. "I'm not going, so leave me alone."

"Come on, Whit," he whined, wedging himself against the doorframe to prevent me from locking him out of the guest room, putting us in close proximity. Close enough that I could see just how long his eyelashes were, see that his brown eyes had tiny flecks of gold in them. "It'll be good for you."

"I've told you a million times to stop calling me Whit."

"It's just the Nest," he teased. "Clean, wholesome fun. Even a prude like you couldn't object."

"Ha ha. You're so funny."

"Seriously. Why won't you come?"

"I don't feel like being on everyone's Facebook News Feed tomorrow, thanks," I said, trying to push the door shut.

He blocked it, squeezing himself all the way into the room and brushing past me without an invitation.

"Christ, do you realize how rude that is?"

"So you're telling me," he said, plopping down on the bed, "that you're going to stay home and be a hermit for the rest of the summer because you're scared that some bored moron might write a comment about you on Facebook?" He rolled his eyes. "Come on."

"It's more than just that group," I said, ignoring him. "It's the people who've read those stories. Everyone in this god-damn town knows my name, and they all think I'm some filthy slut."

"Then prove them wrong."

"I'm not going, Nathan. Drop it."

"Please, Whit. Don't make me bring Bailey in here."

"What does she have to do with this?" I asked.

"She's the one who wants to go," he said. "She's been dying to go all week, but she didn't want to pressure you, since you'd been so down. I told her I'd talk you into it. This is all her idea."

I was surprised. Bailey had spent the last couple of months avoiding the social scene, backing out whenever I invited her to go to the Nest with Harrison and me. It made sense — for her to be scared, I mean. I figured it would be a long time before she got back on the horse.

I underestimated her.

"I'll bring Bailey in here," Nathan threatened. "We both know you can't say no to her."

"Yes, I can."

"No, you really can't."

I rolled my eyes and slumped against the wall. "Why do I have to go? Why can't you take her and leave me here?"

"Because she wants you there," he said. "And so do I."

Those last four words shouldn't have made my heart rate speed up a notch, but they did.

"No," I mumbled, feeling myself start to waver.

"Whitley, is this about Harrison's party?" His voice was quiet.

I wrapped my arms around myself. Phantom breath and ghost fingers lingering on my skin. "I can't, Nathan," I whispered. "It was my fault with Theo that night. If I hadn't gotten so drunk and gone with him, if I hadn't let everyone think —"

"No, Whit. That was *not* your fault."

"If I hadn't —"

"I'm going to keep telling you this until you believe me," he said. "I don't care what you think you did. No one deserves that. *No one.* That guy was a sick bastard — a complete asshole. You did *not* ask for it. So stop blaming yourself."

I looked down. "I just don't want to go out tonight, all right?"

"Listen to me." He stood up and walked across the room to stand in front of me, putting his hand on my shoulder. "I know you've been having a rough time lately. With your dad and all that. I know that what happened at Harrison's party scared you. I'm sorry about everything."

"Don't go all Hallmark on me," I warned, focusing on a

231

small tear in the collar of his plain navy T-shirt instead of looking him in the face.

"Look, I'm glad that you've chilled out a little lately — easing up on the Girls Gone Wild act — but you're just going to make yourself miserable staying in here."

"Girls Gone Wild? Please. You only wish I'd taken my shirt off."

Oh, wait. I *had* taken my top off in front of him. On graduation night *and* that one time in his car outside of the movie rental store. Whoops.

He pretended not to hear me.

"You need to get out. Have a little fun. You *can* have fun without tequila, you know. I swear."

"Christ, Nathan, can't you just drop it?" I asked, trying to swerve out of his reach.

He caught my other shoulder and pushed me lightly against the wall again. Finally, I looked up at him. He stared down into my face as he held me between his hands. We were standing too close. For a minute, all the feelings I'd been trying to stifle came bubbling to the surface. I was looking right into his eyes; I could smell his fresh, cinnamon breath. All I wanted was to kiss him. Or for him to kiss me. It didn't matter.

But that wasn't what this was about.

"I want you to be happy," he said. "And we both know you're not happy like this. Locking yourself in here isn't going to make you happy. It's not going to make any of us happy."

"Nathan..."

"Either you promise me right now that you'll come with us," he insisted, "or I'll go get Bailey and have her lay those puppy eyes on you. We both know you're wrapped around her little finger. You'd do anything if she asked."

I knew he was right.

But in that moment, as I opened my mouth to answer, a scary realization hit me: Everything he'd just said about Bailey applied to him, too. I'd do almost anything for this boy.

"Fine," I relented. Then, with a forced smile, I added, "I mean, it looks like you actually combed your hair. We wouldn't want that rare effort going to waste."

He laughed as I thumped him on the side of the head with my index finger. His soft brown hair — which really did look neater than usual — tickled my knuckle. God, I wanted to run my fingers through it. Luckily, he was stepping away, removing the temptation. At least a little bit.

Silently, I reminded myself that I couldn't feel anything beyond friendship for Nathan Caulfield. He was going to be my stepbrother. It would be weird. People would think...lots of things.

I wasn't allowed to like him.

It might have been my imagination, but the minute we walked into the Nest, I could have sworn that every pair of eyes turned to look at me. The girls were giving me cold, disapproving glares. The boys smirked menacingly, spotting their prey. I folded in on myself, scooting closer to Nathan. I wanted to leave already.

People had thought of me as a slut back home. I was a party girl, a wild child, a bad influence. But things are different in cities, I guess. Because in the city, there are plenty of other sluts. Plenty of other people to gossip about. And there was a chance that the new people you met had never heard of you. I mean, I graduated with people — Nathan, for instance — that I'd never met.

Hamilton wasn't the city. Here, I was a hot topic.

"I don't think..." I began, already stumbling backward in an attempt to get to the exit.

"Smile," Nathan muttered near my ear. "We're here to have a good time, remember?"

I looked at Bailey and realized how pathetic I was. Four years younger than me, and she was standing there with her head high, like she belonged there.

"I'm going to go dance," she said.

"You are?" I asked, shocked.

"Of course she is," Nathan said. "Dancing is fun. We should dance, too, Whit."

I shook my head. There were so many reasons not to dance with Nathan. The biggest being my already-damaged reputation. Bumping and grinding with my soon-to-be stepbrother wouldn't earn me any brownie points.

Bailey ran off to dance while I pushed my way toward the very, very back of the club. I slid into a booth, checking over my shoulder for camera phones aimed my way.

"Smile," Nathan said again, sliding into the seat across from me.

"I don't want to," I snapped. "Why did you force me to come here?"

He ignored that question. "Smile, Whit. Make them think there is no place you'd rather be."

"But —"

"Smile."

I forced an obnoxious grin onto my lips.

"Happy now?" I asked through gritted teeth. "I'm smiling, goddamn it."

"Good," he said. "Keep at it."

"Oh my God, there you are!"

I looked up just as Harrison plopped down in the booth. He winked at Nathan before turning to face me. "So, the intervention worked," he said, sneaking his arm around my shoulder and squeezing. "I knew you couldn't say no to Nathan."

"Intervention? What are you...?" I turned to glare at Nathan.

"Harrison and I both agreed that you needed to get out of the house," Nathan said.

"You said it was Bailey's idea," I snapped.

"She was in on it, too."

I looked back and forth between them, letting the air hiss between my teeth. "So, you two were plotting against me... together?"

"Something like that," Nathan said, shrugging. He looked to Harrison. "Take her out on the dance floor. She won't dance with me."

"No."

"Yes!" Harrison exclaimed, grabbing my wrist and dragging me out of the booth. He was pretty freaking strong. No wonder he'd beaten the shit out of Theo so easily. "I want to see that cute little ass shaking right now. You can't fight the music, baby!"

"You are *so* gay," I said, just as he spun me around to face him. We were in the middle of the dance floor now, surrounded by a million bodies, all bouncing and swaying... and looking at me. I tried not to think about that as Harrison pulled me closer to him, his hands on my hips, forcing me to move. The truth was, I could dance. I really could. But this was too much. For the first time ever, I was feeling claustrophobic.

"Harrison, I'm not in the mood for this."

"I can't hear you!" he shouted over the loud techno music, but I knew he could. "Dance, sweetie. Just dance."

Without warning, he twirled me around, catching me again easily.

He was a good dancer, too.

Just then, Bailey danced past us. Her long golden hair whipped around her shoulders, and her arms waved over her head. She was alone, but smiling. Laughing, even. She was the most beautiful I'd ever seen her.

I smiled. Seeing her enjoying herself so much, so unafraid — it made me happier than I'd been in a long time.

I took a breath and rolled my shoulders, telling myself to relax. I let Harrison twirl and dip me, let him dance me around the floor, let myself enjoy it. After a while, Nathan cut in and Harrison went to dance with Bailey. I cared about the three of them, and they cared about me. Cared about me enough to put up with my shit, enough to drag me out of the house when I'd been a wallowing hermit for the past few weeks.

I'd poured out the bottle of tequila because I didn't want to keep hurting them, but closing myself off had been hurting me, and they wouldn't let that happen. They loved me no matter what the rest of the world thought. I couldn't just stop being afraid, but for them, I could try.

26

Bailey twirled her way into the house, her hips still shimmying to the beat of a song that had faded away when we left the Nest fifteen minutes earlier.

Nathan and I watched her, neither of us saying a word. I guess we were afraid to take her off cloud nine. She'd danced the entire night — with Nathan, Harrison, and me in turns. And it had been a blast.

We'd both overcome some fears that night, I thought.

"Okay," she sang, bouncing toward the stairs. "Good night. I'm going to bed." Then she was gone in a whirl of blond hair and body glitter.

Nathan looked at me and shook his head. "How can she sleep?" he asked. "She's the Energizer Bunny tonight."

"She probably wore herself out, though," I told him as we climbed the stairs, keeping our voices down. It was past midnight (Sylvia had extended Bailey's curfew just this once), so the adults were asleep. "All that dancing. She'll crash as soon as she hits the mattress."

"Well, at least she had a good time," he said. Then he grinned at me. "And it looked like you did, too. Thank God. I was starting to worry. Your hermit ways were getting out of hand. I mean, you were starting to smell and —"

"Shut up. I was not."

He laughed. "Sure you weren't."

I elbowed him hard in the ribs as we rounded the corner into the guest room. "Don't make me kick your ass."

"I'm terrified." Nathan sat down on the bed, beaming at me. "Seriously, I'm glad you had fun tonight. Harrison and I really were worried."

"Thank you," I said, reaching up and pulling the ponytail holder out of my hair. "I'm glad you guys got me to go out. I needed that push."

"We just want you to be happy, Whit."

"I know," I said. "Which is why I've decided to stop wallowing and try to enjoy the rest of my summer. Because no matter what happens with Dad, I have friends. I'm not alone. And that's what counts, right?"

"Sounds like dirty dancing with Harrison clarified some things for you," he said. "Maybe I should try it sometime."

I snorted. "Harrison would love that! No, seriously, he would. He has a crazy crush on you."

"Really?"

"Yep."

"Wow. I'm flattered."

"You should be," I said, glancing at myself in the mirror over the dresser. "He's a sexy beast. You'd be a lucky man."

"I'm sure I would be." He laughed.

I turned back to Nathan, smiling. "College starts in just over two weeks. I know I'll see you there, but I don't have much summer left to spend with Bailey and Harrison. So I'm going to take advantage of it. Fuck Dad. Fuck the people in this town. They're not going to ruin this for me, goddamn it."

"Beautiful speech," he said, raising his hands and clapping them together. "Bravo."

"Oh, stop that." I reached forward and grabbed his wrists, pulling his hands apart. "You are such a moron."

He was smiling, laughing. His skin was warm beneath my palms. Suddenly, those feelings overcame me again. The urges I'd been experiencing since the aloe incident. The emotions I'd realized the night we watched movies in his bedroom. I'd been working hard to fight them off, but...

His lips pulled into a smirk, sending a tingly feeling down my spine.

"Oh, screw it," I whispered.

I leaned down, pushing his arms out of the way, and kissed him. His lips were soft against mine. Tender. Without even realizing it, I moved onto the bed, straddling his lap. His hands broke free of my grip and moved to press against my back, pulling me into him, even as the kiss remained gentle and slow.

For a minute, it was perfect.

"Whitley," he murmured against my mouth, breathless. "We can't do this."

"Shh..." I pressed in closer, my arms twisting around his neck. "It's okay. It doesn't matter what anyone thinks."

I kissed him again, so hard this time that he fell backward against the pillows, with me landing on top of him. He wanted me, too. I could tell by the way he kissed me back, his lips parting, his tongue finally sliding next to mine. It sent a surge of excitement rippling through my limbs. My heart started racing, and as my fingers moved down his chest, I could feel that his was, too.

It felt so good to give in to temptation. To have his careful hands gliding over me. Not pawing or grabbing. Not greedy. They slid down my back, up my sides, curled in my hair. Slow, lingering touches.

My head began to spin. My whole body felt alive, like it was on fire. I gasped for breath between each kiss, my fingers digging into his soft cotton T-shirt. Something like euphoria swept over me, and I couldn't think about anything anymore. It was just Nathan and me and way too many layers of clothing between us. I wanted to touch every inch of him. I wanted to melt into him. I *wanted* him. So much.

But Nathan's hand moved to my shoulder, and without warning he pushed me up, away from him.

"No," he panted. "I can't do this, Whit."

"Nathan," I whined. "We're not actually related. It isn't weird, okay? Please, just —"

241

"That's not it," he said, rolling me off him and sitting up on the bed.

I propped myself on an elbow, frustrated. "Then what the hell is your problem?" I demanded. "Seriously, Nathan. I've thrown myself at you twice, and you shut me down both times. I know you want me, too."

"That's just it," he said, standing up and walking across the room. "I want you...more of you than you're willing to give."

"More than I'm...?" I frowned, getting to my knees on the mattress. "What are you talking about?"

He turned to face me, his hand already on the doorknob. "I told you. I don't want to be that kind of guy. I don't just want sex, Whit. I want more. I want everything. I want *you*."

"Nathan..."

"I'm not settling for less, Whitley," he said. "And neither should you."

And he walked out of the room.

For a minute, I was pissed. Really pissed. He wanted *everything*, but what was everything? I was all over him, willing to do anything in that moment. Anything. What more could he ask for?

Then I remembered what he'd told me in the diner after Harrison's party. He didn't want something cheap. He wanted a girl he liked, a girl he could have a future with. And he wanted me to be that girl. He had since graduation night, since we'd made out in the armchair and I'd named all the songs about blue eyes. Even then, he hadn't just wanted my body. He'd wanted *me*.

And after this summer, after I'd broken his heart, after he'd actually gotten to know me, he hadn't changed his mind. I fell backward onto the pillows. Dumb, dumb, dumb.

It took me a long time to stand up, but I did. There was something I had to do. Something I'd been afraid to attempt for weeks. But, finally, I felt like I could do it.

I knelt down next to my duffel bag and began pulling out the wrinkled clothes, folding them up and placing them one by one in the drawers of the oak dresser.

My dresser. In *my* bedroom.

People cared about me here. Nathan, Bailey, Sylvia — I'd given them every reason in the world to hate me, but they didn't. They'd tried so hard to make me feel welcome in this house, even when Dad had ignored me. And slowly, I'd come to care about them, too. Maybe I didn't fit in, but they were willing to make room for me here. And I was ready to take them up on that.

27

"Enjoying your stay at your dad's?"

"Yeah."

"Been spending time with him and his new family?"

"Uh-huh."

"You like them?"

"Yes. Very much."

Mom and I hadn't spoken in weeks, and the one time I actually answered her call, she started digging. For insults. For bitch fits. For anything negative about Dad. It was the morning after I'd unpacked, after I'd decided I belonged here with these people. And Mom was reminding me exactly why I felt more comfortable here than in her house.

"I bet you see them more than you see your father, don't you?" she scoffed. "Good God. I mean, you've known them for five minutes, and he's already leaving you alone with them all the time, I'd imagine. What if they're psychos or something?"

"They're not."

"You don't know that, Whitley. Your father has never had good judgment."

"Mom, they're fine," I snapped. "I like them, okay? Drop it."

Silence. I'd shut her up. But only for a second.

"Honey, is something wrong?" Mom asked. "You sound upset. What's the matter? You can tell me."

"No," I said through gritted teeth. "No, Mom, I can't tell you. I can't tell you that Dad and I barely speak to each other. Or that I think he likes his new family more than me. Or that it hurts because I love his family, too. I can't tell you. I can't tell you *anything* because all you do is bitch! You bitch and bitch and bitch about Dad. All the time."

Hot tears were burning in the corners of my eyes. I tried to fight them. This was dumb. Crying on the phone with Mom was stupid and dumb. Because it wasn't as if she gave a shit. Not about my feelings.

"Whitley —"

"Shut up," I growled. "Just shut up. Hearing you complain about Dad isn't helping me. It hasn't helped me for the past six goddamn years. All you think about is him. How much you hate him. How much he's hurt you. But you forget that *I* love him, that sometimes I'm like him. And I'm still *here*! So just *shut up* and think about someone else for a change. Like your own fucking daughter."

There was silence again. This time, she didn't break it.

I took a few deep breaths, rubbing my eyes with the back of my wrist. I couldn't believe I'd just done it. I'd said all of the things I'd been thinking for years. But I hadn't meant to. They just poured out. Gushed from my lips without my permission. Now that it was out there, though, it was kind of a relief.

And kind of terrifying.

"Mom, I have to go. I'll talk to you later."

I hung up before she could say another word.

Bailey's cheerleading tryouts that week were a family event. Sylvia even took off work to make it to the three o'clock session. Though, in reality, there wasn't much to do or see. Dad, Sylvia, Nathan, and I mostly just stood out in the high school's ugly orange-and-blue hallway, waiting with our fingers crossed as Bailey and two dozen other girls auditioned behind the closed gymnasium doors.

I tried not to feel bitter. I mean, my dad only saw me two and a half months out of the year, and he barely noticed me then, yet he was going to his not-even-stepdaughter's cheerleading tryouts. Tryouts he couldn't actually witness. But, yeah, I did my best to push that feeling away. This was Bailey's day, and being selfish would make me both a crappy friend and sister.

Sylvia twitched nervously beside me, letting out her breath in long, low bursts. Her foot tapped against the tile floor, and she stared straight ahead, unable to be distracted by the rest of us. Christ, she was more stressed about this than Bailey had been. Just looking at her made me anxious.

"So, Nate, did you watch the game last night?"

I glanced to my left. Dad was trying to distract himself. That or make up for the boredom of standing in this ugly-ass hallway. Either way, he was employing Nathan. His new son. The athlete he'd always wanted. Nathan was going to his old college, playing his favorite sport, doing all the things he'd urged Trace and me to do.

No wonder he didn't need us anymore. He had the child he'd always hoped for now.

My eyes slid over to Nathan, standing on the other side of my father. His hands were shoved deep in his pockets, and his foot bounced in the same rhythm as Sylvia's. For a second, he met my gaze, and I had to turn away.

Things had been weird for us since the kiss a few nights ago....Well, weird for me, at least. Nathan went on like everything was normal. Smiling at me. Laughing with me. Making his usual jokes and comments. Like we hadn't made out yet again. Like we were still just friends or stepsiblings or whatever the hell we had been. Like nothing had changed.

And I guess, technically, nothing had.

Not for him, anyway.

But for me, everything about our relationship had changed. I'd been kind of confused before — lusting after your soon-to-be stepbrother is really awkward and all — but now...now it was so much worse. Because ever since he'd left my bedroom Friday night, I'd been thinking about what he had said. The things he'd implied.

He wanted me.

247

And I was pretty sure I wanted him, too.

Believe me, falling for your future stepbrother is way, way more confusing than simply wanting to jump his bones.

I didn't know if I should tell him how I felt, though. Tell him that I'd grown to want a relationship, a commitment, and that I wanted it with him. Part of me knew I had to. Because ignoring my feelings and letting him slip through my fingers could only lead me to a lot of regret. To be honest, I'd never felt this way about a guy before. I'd be an idiot to let him get away.

On the other hand, I was scared. Really scared.

Not just of this whole relationship idea — though that was a new concept for me — but of what it might do to my family.

My family. The Caulfields had become my family. Even if Mom and Dad were clueless and Trace had moved on, I still had the Caulfields. And I didn't want to mess that up.

I hadn't made up my mind yet. And, in the meantime, just making eye contact with Nathan made me jittery. Made the confusion roll over in my stomach and settle into my belly like a pound of lead. I couldn't pretend it wasn't there. I couldn't live like this much longer.

I needed to decide on something soon.

"Yeah, the game was good," I heard him tell Dad, but I could have sworn I felt his eyes pressing into the back of my head. "Two extra innings. Pretty intense."

"Oh, here they come," Sylvia gasped as the gym doors swung open. Her hand immediately grabbed hold of mine, squeezing it like I was her own personal stress ball.

"Ow."

"Sorry," she murmured, loosening her grip a little. "I'm just so..."

"Me, too." I squeezed back and smiled at her. "It's fine."

One by one, the auditioning girls exited the gymnasium, all in varying states of excitement or dejection. A few even came into the hallway with full-blown tears streaking their cheeks, and they ran instantly into the arms of their waiting parents. Christ, I hoped Bailey wouldn't be like that. I couldn't take crying. Especially if it was from her. I'd be tempted to go in and kick the preppy blond judges' asses.

"Here she is," Dad said, stepping up beside me as Bailey came out of the gym, an unreadable expression on her face. "How'd it go, Bailey-Boop?"

Bailey didn't say anything. She looked at each of us for a moment, not quite a smile but not quite a frown on her face.

Finally, Bailey moved. She walked straight toward me and, without warning, wrapped her arms around my torso in one of the tightest hugs I'd ever experienced. She almost squeezed the breath out of me. She was pretty strong for such a skinny kid.

"Um... Bailey?" I said, patting her uncertainly on the back. I was afraid she was going to start crying into my cotton T-shirt. "What... ?"

"Thank you," she said. After a second, she let go, her face glowing with pride. "Thank you, thank you, thank you! I MADE IT!" She did a little jump in the air and touched her toes — probably something she'd used in her tryout — and let out a whoop so loud I thought I heard the ceiling tiles rattle. "I made it! I made it! They picked me!"

"We heard you the first time," Nathan said.

"But once is *so* not good enough," she countered. She turned to face me again, her eyes shining with excitement. "Thank you, Whitley. I couldn't have done it without you. You really helped me with my routine these past couple weeks."

"Bailey, I just sat there and watched you," I reminded her, reaching out to ruffle her hair. "You did all the work, kid."

"Congratulations, baby!" Sylvia exclaimed, throwing her arms around Bailey.

"I'm so proud of you, Boop," Dad said, patting the top of her head. "Great job."

I'm not jealous, I told myself. *I'm happy. Happy for Bailey. Screw Dad. This is about her, not him.*

Bailey looked embarrassed, her cheeks turning bright pink.

"Oh, what the hell!" Nathan said, tossing a wink at me, Harrison-style. "Group hug in Bailey's honor."

"You're not serious," I muttered.

"Oh, no, Nathan. Please —" Bailey tried, but it was too late.

Nathan collapsed onto her, his arms encircling his sister and mother. Dad followed suit within seconds, and it was my father's hand that grabbed my arm, pulling me into this hideous display of affection. His arm wrapped around my shoulders, squishing me into the group.

"God, you guys, stop it!" she shrieked beneath us. "This is so embarrassing. People can see."

I would have agreed with her. Normally, at least. I would have run from awkward, weird, sentimental things like this. Screaming, most likely. But suddenly, this felt less disgusting and more . . . real. Solid. *Right.*

With Dad on one side of me, his arm around my shoulder, and Sylvia and Nathan and Bailey, all of us squished together, all of us connected, it felt okay. Good, even.

I felt Nathan's hand reach out for me, his palm moving to the small of my back. Like a reminder. Or maybe a reassurance.

These people were my family. They'd be here for me no matter what. No matter what people said, what mistakes I made . . . or who I fell for.

And just then, I made up my mind.

The paper felt hot between my fingers. Slick, too. Probably wet from the sweat on my palms. So gross. But whatever. I wasn't backing out now. Not when I was this close.

My fist clenched around the Post-it as I knocked on Nathan's bedroom door with my other hand. My heartbeat sped up dramatically, and for a minute I thought I might have a nervous breakdown. This should not have been so hard. I mean, I'd been talking to guys for years. Flirting with them. Hooking up with them. This should have been easy.

"Come in."

I exhaled and pushed open the door. He was sitting on his bed, wearing a *Battlestar Galactica* T-shirt and reading an

X-Men comic book. I couldn't help smiling a little, despite my nervousness. Who would have guessed that a nerd would be the one to rope me in? A hot nerd, but still definitely a nerd.

"Hey," he said, putting the comic aside. "What's up?"

"I...um..." I looked down at my clenched fist. The yellow corners of the note poked out between my fingers. "It's about the other night. What you said...in my room."

"Oh." He sounded surprised. I looked up to find him staring at me, his eyes wide. He shifted, sitting up a bit straighter. Like he was just as anxious as I was. How ridiculous was this? We both knew rejection wasn't waiting for us. We both knew how the other felt — because I was sure he could see right through me. So why was this so scary?

I looked down at my feet, avoiding his gaze. "I...well, here." I tossed the Post-it onto the bed like it was scalding my flesh or something. I was so eager to get it out of my hand. So eager to have everything out in the open.

He leaned over to pick up the crumpled piece of paper, and I waited with bated breath as he read. Waited...waited...

"I don't get it."

Goddamn it. Of course he didn't.

"Think about it," I insisted.

"It's your cell number," he said, staring down at the yellow square of paper. "Whit, I already have your number. It's programmed into my phone. Why do I need —"

"It's a *symbol*," I groaned, rolling my eyes. "Come on, Nathan. Don't make me say it."

He read over the digits a few more times before I finally

saw a light flicker behind his eyes, and he looked up at me, that familiar smile spreading across his face. "So, you...?"

"Yeah," I said, exasperated. "Why else would I be here?"

Before another word could escape either of our throats, he slid off the bed and walked toward me. It felt so natural as his arms wrapped around my waist and he pulled me into him. Like we *fit* together. It all came so easily. The way his lips found mine, even with both our eyes closed. The way his palm seemed to meld perfectly against my back. The way my arms fit around his shoulders. Like pieces of a puzzle, and this time I belonged.

In a lot of ways, this was my first kiss. My first real one, at least. The first one that actually meant something. It was everything I'd hoped for at Bailey's age. Before the parties and the boys got involved. The kind of greedless kiss I never really thought I would find.

But here it was. Right in the middle of what, up until very recently, I'd considered the worst summer of my life.

Maybe it wasn't such a nightmare after all.

The photos didn't stop popping up on Facebook. Ever since the night at the Nest when I'd finally decided to ignore the stupid shit people were saying about me, I hadn't checked the page or even asked Nathan about it. I didn't want to care about it anymore. Still, Sylvia had pulled me aside after dinner one night to check in.

"Are you okay? I know the page is still up. Are you sure you don't want me to pursue this, Whitley?"

"I'm fine," I said. And, for the most part, I meant it. "It probably was cyber-bullying, but I've stopped letting it get to me, so I'm pretty over it."

She nodded and touched my arm. "I'm glad, but let me know if you change your mind. I just want to be sure you're okay."

And, really, I was. Nathan, Bailey, Harrison — they'd all shown me that it wasn't important what the idiots in this town thought of me. They loved me, and that's what mattered.

As Sylvia walked away, though, I wished she hadn't been the one talking to me about this. It had always been her. But it needed to be Dad. I wanted him to discuss the issue with me instead of just blowing it off.

The next morning, after a new picture appeared online, I got my wish. Just not in the way I'd hoped.

The photo had been taken at the Nest. On Tuesday night, the day after Bailey's tryouts, Nathan, Harrison, and I had decided to take her out to celebrate.

As soon as we got to the Nest, the four of us found a booth close to the dance floor. Bailey was bouncing up and down excitedly, her little white sandals tapping along to the music. I didn't think she'd stopped smiling since the tryouts. And it was pretty goddamn contagious. We all had grins smeared across our faces because of her.

"Bailey, sweetie, I love your dress," Harrison said as he slipped into the booth beside her. "You can really pull off pastels. I'm so freaking jealous."

"Thanks."

"You know," I said to her, "Harrison is a real fashionista. He'd probably be good help on that shopping spree you were talking about earlier. The one after your birthday? If you're still up for it, I mean."

"Um, of course I am!" she said. "Harrison, my birthday is this Monday. Can we go shopping sometime that week? Before Whitley leaves on Friday? You have to come."

"Shopping? I'll be there." He looked across the table to Nathan. "You coming with us, babe?"

I couldn't help but smile at Nathan's lack of reaction to being called "babe" by another male. Any other guy might have freaked out. Or at least raised an eyebrow. It didn't seem to faze him, though.

"Bailey doesn't want me picking her clothes," he said. "I'd be trying to put her in turtlenecks and long pants all year long. Hiding as much skin as possible." He nodded at his sister. "I don't like how short that little cheerleading skirt is, either."

"You'll get over it," she replied.

"I doubt that."

"Come on, sweetie," Harrison said, grabbing Bailey's wrist. "Dance with me. Let's show everyone in this club those moves you've got. We'll have every straight boy in Hamilton *begging* for your number by the end of the night."

Bailey let him drag her onto the floor, giggling the whole way.

I laughed and turned to smile at Nathan.

He looked worried.

"What?" I asked.

"I don't know if I like the idea of every boy in Hamilton chasing my sister," he said. "I have the sudden urge to lock her in a closet...until she's twenty-five."

"Well, look on the bright side," I said, squeezing his hand. "There aren't *that* many boys in Hamilton. Only about...two hundred or so? You can fight off two hundred, can't you?"

"Of course I can," he scoffed. "See these muscles? I work out, remember? I'd just rather not have to. The closet idea seems easier."

I grinned at him, my fingers trailing up his arm. It felt good to be allowed to do this, to touch him without feeling embarrassed or guilty. "You know," I whispered, leaning in, "you could lock me in your closet. I wouldn't mind."

Nathan's worried expression turned into a sly smile that matched mine. "Oh, is that so?"

"Yeah." I licked my lips, shifting so that my thigh was pressed close against his.

He looked down at our legs, shaking his head. "You know," he said, resting a hand on my knee. "That little move? It doesn't work every time. Not all boys are that easy."

"It worked on you once, didn't it?" I moved in closer so I could kiss him.

It was innocent. No groping. No hands sliding under my shirt. There wasn't even tongue, for God's sake. It was just a kiss.

But it changed everything.

Because as his hand moved up my arm to touch my hair and my eyes slid shut, neither of us noticed the camera phone pointed our way. Neither of us had a clue that we were being watched.

At least, not until Dad slammed his laptop down in front

of me while I ate breakfast the next morning, his face beet red and his eyes practically popping out of his skull.

"What the hell is this?" he demanded, jabbing a finger at the screen. "Start talking, Whitley."

I glanced at the monitor and realized I was staring at Dad's Facebook page. At the very top was a new post. *Greg Johnson has been tagged in a photo*. My eyes found the image, and as I looked it over for a moment, I actually had to think about why he was angry. It was just a picture of Nathan and me. To be honest, it was kind of cute. Well shot. It looked a bit like a screenshot from a romantic movie. One of those perfect kisses.

"What's the problem?" I asked.

"Damn it, Whitley." His fist hit the table so hard that my cereal bowl shook.

I flinched.

"What the hell are you and Nathan doing? Why are you kissing him?"

And then I got it.

Dad didn't know about Nathan and me yet.

No one did. Well, except Harrison...and Bailey, if she'd managed to figure it out on her own, which I was sure she had, since we weren't doing much to hide our relationship now.

"We're dating," I said, picking up my spoon.

"No, you most certainly are not," Dad snapped, making me flinch again.

We were the only ones in the kitchen. Nathan was at the gym. Sylvia had taken Bailey shopping for a new pair of athletic tennis shoes. And I'd only just rolled out of bed at eleven in the morning. I'd been halfway through my breakfast when Dad stormed out of his study, laptop in hand.

Now I wished I'd gotten up early. Gone shopping with Sylvia and Bailey, or even to the gym with Nathan. Anything to avoid this conversation. Which clearly wasn't going to go very well.

"How could you do this?" he asked, still furious.

"Do what?" I asked. "I didn't do anything."

"I want you to end things with Nathan," he said. "Whatever is going on with you two, I want you to put a stop to it right now."

"No."

"Don't argue with me, young lady."

I stood up so fast that my chair toppled over behind me. "No!" I was the angry one now. "We aren't doing anything wrong. We're just dating. It's not like he's actually my brother, so why should I have to end it?"

"Because I said so," he snarled.

"That's not a good enough reason."

"Don't talk back to me like that," he said, his palms smacking the table again. He leaned forward, his eyes burning into mine. "You are my daughter, and this is *my* house. You will do as I say. You won't see Nathan. You won't date him or kiss him or do whatever it is you two are doing. And that is final."

He straightened up and turned around, ready to leave the room.

"No," I said again.

He stopped in the doorway to the living room. "Whitley," he growled.

"No," I repeated.

In a sick way, I was glad we were fighting. Glad he was yelling at me, paying attention to me. But now he was walking away. Not even listening to me. Not even bothering to hear my side of the story. I thought I might do anything to keep him in the room. Even fling myself on the ground and throw a tantrum like a two-year-old. Whatever it took to keep him here. To make him turn around. To make him see me.

And I thought the way to make him stay was to say something dramatic. Something that would shock him. Only, the words that came to mind happened to be the truth.

"I'm falling in love with him," I said. "I'm not going to stop seeing him. I won't."

"Then pack your things."

"What?"

"I'll have someone fill in for me at the station, and I'll take you back to your mom's tomorrow afternoon," he said, his back still to me. "I won't deal with this behavior in my home."

And he left the room.

It didn't sink in at first. I sat down, my eyes on Dad's laptop. I clicked the picture, read the caption: *Whitley seems to have a thing for brotherly love.*

"Fuck them," I said quietly. "Fuck them. They don't matter."

But Dad did.

He mattered because he could take them away. Nathan, Bailey, Sylvia, Harrison — he could take away the only people who cared about me. The words sank in slowly. I was basically being kicked out.

Kicked out of my home.

At the beginning of the summer, I swore this place would never become my home, but it had. I didn't realize it until now, until it was being taken away, and yet, somehow, this house felt safer, more real, than my mother's house in Indiana ever had. The Caulfields had made this my home.

I didn't want to leave.

I ran upstairs, hot tears stinging my eyes and burning the tops of my cheeks. I pushed open the door of the guest room — *my* room — and threw myself onto the bed — *my* bed.

I just lay there for a while, my face in the pillow, trying to calm down. When my heartbeat finally slowed, I rolled onto my back and stared at the ceiling. My head hurt. My stomach ached. Dad's decision to send me back to Mom's house put me in a serious state of pain. What was I supposed to do? I didn't want to go back. I didn't want to leave now. I had a week and a half left here. A week and a half left with Nathan. With the Caulfields. With my family.

Not anymore.

The house was eerily empty around me now. Dad was somewhere downstairs, I knew, but the TV was off. And the others hadn't come back yet.

I needed to talk to someone. I needed advice.

I reached over to the nightstand and picked up my cell phone. The screen flashed one missed call from Mom and a voice mail, but I ignored it. She was the last person I wanted to talk to. We hadn't spoken since our last argument a few days ago, and I was sure she wanted to bitch at me for bitching at her. Whatever. I couldn't deal with her now.

I dialed Trace's house number. L.A. was two hours behind, so I hoped he'd be awake.

"Hello?" Emily's voice said when she answered the phone.

"Um, hey, Em," I said awkwardly. My voice cracked, still not recovered from the crying.

"Whitley? Hey, girl. How are you?"

"Not... not good. Can I talk to Trace, please?"

"Sure. He's playing with Marie right now. She just started laughing for the first time!"

"That's great."

"I know. We're so excited. It's almost ridiculous, I guess. Okay, here's Trace."

The phone crackled as it was passed to my brother, and a second later Trace said, "Hey, sis. What's going on?"

"I have a problem," I told him. "And I really just need you to listen and tell me what to do."

"Oh-*kay*," Trace said. "I'll do my best."

I took a deep breath, let it out, and started talking.

I told him everything. About Dad. About the Caulfields. About Nathan, the graduation party (in minimal detail), and Facebook. Trace never interrupted. He just listened until I got it all out. Listened while I ranted and nearly started crying again and wallowed in self-pity. He listened and listened until I finally got out the last few words of my story.

"...and now he wants to send me back to Mom's, and I don't want to go. What do I do, Trace?"

"Wow," he said. "Seriously — *wow*. I mean, what are the odds that of all the people Dad might marry, the chick's son is someone you've —"

"Trace!"

"Sorry. Okay, advice...hmm."

I waited through his thoughtful pause, half expecting him to tell me that the best plan would be to just end things with Nathan. Logically, that probably seemed like the solution, but I couldn't. And I shouldn't have to.

I guess Trace knew that, because he said, "Really, Whitley, all you can do is try to talk to Dad again."

"About what?"

"About how you feel," Trace said. "You should talk to him and to Mom. You clearly have issues with both of them, and who knows? Maybe just telling them how you feel could fix things. Or at least improve them a little."

"I doubt it."

"Well, I don't know what else to tell you," he said. "I'm sorry. I hate that you're having to deal with this."

"Yeah, it sucks."

"You'll figure it out," Trace said. "Just do whatever will make you happy. That's what's important. Don't forget that, okay?"

"Whatever."

Everyone said that to me. That they wanted me to be happy. That it was the most important thing. But just when I started to figure out what I wanted — what would make me happy — it was squashed.

Talk about goddamn mixed messages.

"Hey, don't 'whatever' me," he said. "I mean it. I'm sorry my advice is unoriginal, but I'll do whatever I can to help. I could call Dad if you want. Make him listen to me. Or Mom. If you can't talk to them, I can."

"No." I sighed. "That's okay. You don't have to."

There was a short silence before Trace said, "I'm sorry, Whitley. I know you've been having a horrible summer, and I haven't been there for you as much as I should have. I've just been so —"

"Busy," I said. "I know. It's fine. You have a family to worry about now."

"You *are* my family," he said.

The tears almost started up again. Those four little words meant so much to me — which was stupid, really. They were just words. But they were words I'd been wanting to hear, wanting to believe. *You are my family.*

"You sure you don't want me to call Dad?" Trace asked.

"I'm sure," I said. "Really. I don't think there's anything anyone can do."

"Okay," he said. "But call me if you need me. I'll be here."

As I hung up the phone, I tried to comfort myself with that thought. Trace would be there. He wouldn't judge me or

264

abandon me. Even if I lost Dad. Even if I never fixed things with Mom. Even if my relationship with Nathan didn't work out and I screwed things up with the Caulfields, I had Trace. He was my family.

But I wasn't sure that would be enough.

Not even a week had passed since I'd finally put my clothes into the drawers of the oak dresser, and here I was, already packing them up again. The thought did cross my mind, how much easier this would've been if I'd just left all of my stuff in the duffel bag. If I'd never unpacked. If I'd never let this place become my home.

Bailey sat at the foot of my bed, watching as I moved sluggishly around the room, my hands clutching one personal belonging or another. She and Sylvia had gotten back home about an hour after my fight with Dad. When Bailey had come upstairs to show me her shoes, she found me still half in tears after my phone call with Trace.

I told her everything. Well, not *everything*. I left out the part about my would-be one-night-stand with Nathan earlier this summer. She was too young to hear that shit. So I started by telling her that we were seeing each other, then worked my way up to this morning in the kitchen with Dad.

She didn't cry, but I could tell she wanted to.

"You know," she said with a weak, forced smile, "I knew there was something going on with you and Nathan."

"Yeah," I said, my laugh sounding strangled and pathetic. "Yeah, you did. Good guess."

"I didn't have to guess," she mumbled, toying with a loose thread in the comforter. "It was pretty obvious."

I shoved a few wrinkled T-shirts into my duffel bag, trying not to think about what I was doing. I focused on Bailey. On what she was saying. On anything but the fact that I was leaving tomorrow afternoon. Because when I thought about how long it might be before I saw her again, it felt like someone was twisting a knife in my gut.

Would Dad let me come to the wedding next month after all of this?

Two months ago, I would have done anything to leave this house. Now, I would have done anything to stay.

The next words Bailey said came out in a half-sobbed whisper: "What about my birthday?"

The knife plunged deeper.

"I'm sorry," I said. "I'm sorry, Bailey. This is my fault. I shouldn't have said . . . Anyway, I'm sure Harrison will take you shopping."

Harrison. Christ, I needed to call him. To tell him why I was going to vanish a week and a half early. But the idea of saying good-bye to him made my eyes sting again. Goddamn it, I wasn't supposed to be a crier, but I'd cried so freaking much this summer.

"I don't want you to leave."

"That makes two of us."

I zipped up my duffel bag.

"Maybe Mom will talk Greg out of sending you home," she said.

"Or maybe she'll be just as upset as he is about Nathan and me dating."

Bailey lowered her head, defeated.

"Hey, guys..."

His voice echoed down the hallway, causing a lump to lodge itself in my throat. *No, no, no,* I thought. Even though I'd be seeing him again soon, at college, telling Nathan I was leaving would be the hardest. Because I knew him. I knew he'd blame himself. And I couldn't handle that right now.

"What's going on?" He poked his head into my room. "Mom and Greg are arguing in their room, and —" He stopped, his eyes scanning my face. "What's wrong?"

I opened my mouth, but the words got lost somewhere behind that knife, which was still carving away at my insides. I looked down at my duffel bag, and I felt his eyes slide down my frame and land on it, too.

"What...?"

"I'll leave you two alone."

Bailey stood up and walked past her brother, edging out the door. She glanced back at me with those sad brown eyes before vanishing into the hallway.

"Whit," he said when she'd gone. "What's going on? Why are you packing again? You don't leave until —"

I was already shaking my head. "No," I said, biting my lip. "I'm leaving tomorrow afternoon. Dad's having someone fill in for him on the news."

"Why?"

"Have you been on Facebook?"

"Not today."

"Well, we're famous." I tried to smile. Tried to pretend it was funny. "Nice picture of you and me at the Nest. Dad was admiring the photographer's handiwork."

Nathan's face went sickly pale. "So…he saw. And he's making you leave because of me."

I shook my head, sinking down onto the bed. "No, it's my fault. I talked back to him, and I think he basically kicked me out." I forced myself to smile when I looked at him. "Because I can drink and sleep around all I want, but it's a mortal sin to kiss the kid whose mom is marrying my dad."

"Stepbrother," he said.

"You're not my stepbrother," I said, exasperated. "Not yet. And don't say it like you think it's wrong, too. We aren't siblings. It isn't *that* weird. And Nathan, I really can't take you blaming yourself or feeling guilty right now, okay?" *No tears, no tears.* I wouldn't. I would not cry again. "I don't want to think that I was wrong, because I know I wasn't. Dad is being an asshole, and that's the end of the story. Please, just be on my fucking side!"

"Hey, hey." Nathan moved forward and sat down on the

269

bed beside me. "Calm down, all right? I am on your side. I'm *always* on your side." He put an arm around me, and I leaned against him, my face buried in his chest.

"I'm sorry," I mumbled into the fabric of his T-shirt. "I just don't get it! He ignored me for the whole summer, and all of a sudden he gives a damn? But instead of fixing it, he's sending me back to Mom's. Why? Why now?"

"I think you should ask him."

I scoffed, pulling away from Nathan. "Yeah, right."

"I'm serious, Whit. You two really need to talk."

"That's what Trace said."

"Well, he's right."

"I get it!" I yelled, pushing Nathan away and standing up. "But I've tried. I have totally tried."

"I know you have," he said. "But right now, you're the only one who can make things better. You're the one who has changed this summer. If you want things to change with your dad, you'll have to be the one to change them."

"I can't."

"Whitley," he said, using that tone that meant he was about to explain something very simple, like I was a five-year-old he had to reason with. "You two will never fix anything if you keep your mouths shut. He's your dad. He loves you."

I snorted. "He likes you better."

"Stop being so melodramatic." Nathan stood up and walked over to stand in front of me, putting his hands on my hips. "Look, I want you to stay. You know I do, but I'll see you in a few weeks at college, and they'll have no say over

270

what we do then. But right now, your dad is the most important thing to worry about. If we have to put our relationship on hold so you two can work things out, I'm fine with that."

"Why do you have to be so damn nice?" I asked, annoyed. "Why can't you get pissed off, too? It would make my life so much easier."

He kissed my forehead — so freaking condescending — and said, with that same old smile, "Because being pissed won't solve anything. Go downstairs and talk to your dad. I'll be here when you're done. Okay?"

"I told you, Trace already suggested that, but it won't work. And besides, I don't want to."

"Yeah, you do." His hands tightened on my hips and he nudged me backward, toward the door. "You really, really do." Then he basically shoved me out of the bedroom, then closed — and *locked* — the door in my face.

I rushed forward, slamming my fist into the wooden door.

"Nathan, this is not cool! Open my freaking door!"

No answer.

Shit. That asshole. He was really going to force me into this. For a minute, I thought about locking myself in *his* room, but I knew that would get us nowhere. Nathan was going to be stubborn about this. Frustrated, I turned around and started down the stairs, knowing I wouldn't be allowed back into my bedroom until I'd had some sort of talk with Dad.

No. Never mind. Technically, it wasn't really my bedroom anymore. It was the guest room again.

I stomped down the stairs, my arms folded tightly over my chest. If I was doing this, I sure as hell wasn't doing it willingly. And Dad was going to know that. He was going to be fully aware of the fact that I hated this whole situation. That Nathan was the one forcing me to speak to him. Which, of course, made him even more of an idiot for trying to split us up, since this probably meant Nathan was a good influence on me.

The words boiled on the tip of my tongue, the angry things I wanted to scream bubbling at the back of my throat. I was ready. If Dad was still going to be an ass about this, I was going to throw a tantrum. A real one. I was going to give him a decent reason to send me packing. I was going to make my effort worth it.

But I hadn't even reached his bedroom door yet when I heard the shouting.

Then I remembered what Nathan had said when he first came into my room a few minutes ago: Dad and Sylvia were fighting.

"You're being unreasonable, Greg."

"Sylvia, I've made up my mind. She's going home."

Oh, great. They were fighting about me.

"Nathan and Whitley have been good for each other. Nathan has gotten so much better this summer, and haven't you noticed the change in Whitley? I don't understand why this is such a big deal to you."

"He's her stepbrother. People will talk."

"Who gives a shit if they talk?"

I froze outside the door, stunned to hear Sylvia's sweet, perky voice using a four-letter word. Of course, I was even more surprised to hear her arguing in my defense.

"Just drop it, Sylvia." Dad sighed.

I could see him through the crack in the door, putting clean clothes in the dresser. The same baby blue shirts and striped ties he always wore. Neat and folded, placed into each drawer. He wasn't even looking at Sylvia, who sat on the bed watching him. And he certainly hadn't noticed me.

What else was new?

"No, I am not going to drop it, Greg." Sylvia stood up suddenly, her hands on her hips. "She's your daughter, and you've barely paid any attention to her all summer."

"That is not true."

"Yeah it is, Dad."

The words had escaped my mouth before I could stop them, and now both Dad's and Sylvia's heads had turned to look at me. I bit my lip, regretting that little slip, but it was too late. They knew I was here. Might as well be out with it. So I pushed open the bedroom door and walked inside.

"Whitley, what are you —"

"She's right, Dad," I said. "Sylvia hit the nail on the head. I've been here all summer and you've barely looked at me."

Fittingly, he wasn't even looking at me now. He'd turned back to his dresser and was folding and putting away shirt after shirt.

"Whitley, this is a private discussion. Please go back upstairs."

I scowled. "Whatever," I muttered, starting to turn around. But the expression I saw on Sylvia's face stopped me. Her eyes were wide, watching me. Begging me to say something. Their shape reminded me of Nathan's, and I remembered that I was locked out of my room.

So I had to try.

Try harder, anyway.

"Dad," I said, forcing the word out. All of the things that had been brewing in my mouth earlier were gone. Not even a trace remained. Like they'd never really been there at all. "Did you see the other pictures?"

"Whitley, I asked you to —"

"Answer her, Greg." Sylvia sounded angry. Really angry. "I've been trying to get you two to talk to each other for weeks. And I'm not letting something as stupid as stubbornness break my family apart. So answer her damn question. She has a right to know."

Dad stayed quiet, still facing the wall, compulsively folding his stupid clothes.

"Why is this such a big deal?" I demanded, taking his silence for a yes. I stepped forward, my fingers curling against my palms.

Part of me wanted to get angry, like Sylvia. To yell and scream like I'd planned. But the logical side of me said that it was a bad idea, that I'd only screw things up even more.

"You didn't care when I was making out with other guys. You didn't care what people thought then. So what does it matter if I kiss Nathan?"

Dad exhaled heavily, finally turning around to face me. He leaned against the dresser, his hands shoved in his pockets. "Whitley, pictures like that just do not reflect well on our family."

"*Our family?*" I laughed bitterly. "I'm your family, too, you know. At least I'm supposed to be. And the other comments and photos definitely didn't reflect well on me. But you never mentioned them. In fact, it only comes up when *Nathan* gets involved."

Dad shook his head. "Whitley."

"No, Dad, I'm serious!" I was embarrassed by how choked the words sounded as they left my throat. My voice was cracking. But I was trying not to lose my cool. I took a breath, lowering my voice a little. "The minute Nathan was pulled into it, you freaked out. You didn't give a shit about my reputation. Just the reputation of your new family. Your new kids. Like I don't fucking matter."

"Oh, honey."

I felt Sylvia's hand graze my shoulder, but I shrugged it away, taking another step closer to Dad. "So, you don't care if everyone thinks I'm a slut, as long as precious Nathan isn't implicated? Why, Dad? Is it because I'm only here in the summer, and you can forget about me the rest of the year? Is it because you've never wanted me? Just like you didn't want me four years ago?" Tears were burning my eyes, and it was taking all my energy to hold them back now. "Or is it just because you like Nathan and Bailey better? Why is it that you can't even bring yourself to give a shit about me?"

Dad looked stunned, and maybe a little hurt. He stepped

toward me, reaching out to touch my arm. "Whitley, I never meant to —"

I moved back, out of his reach. I shook; I was having trouble breathing. Everything I said came out sounding strangled. Pathetic. I was on the verge of sobbing. This wasn't even a tantrum — it was a breakdown. Much less dignified.

"You know what, it's okay," I said. "Because Mom doesn't care, either. Did you know that? Mom still thinks I'm best friends with a girl I haven't spoken to since I was fourteen. She's too busy obsessing over you. That's why I wanted to move in with you four years ago. Because I was *so goddamn miserable*. I had no friends and a mother who couldn't care less, and you didn't even want me."

"Munchkin, I...I'm sorry." His eyes were wide, and I knew he meant it. But I didn't give a shit. Not anymore.

"You should be!" I spluttered. "You see me, like, once a freaking year, and you can't even make time for me then! It's been all about your new family and your perfect wedding. The one time we're actually alone together, you spend the whole day trying on stupid tuxedos. This was *our* summer! The last summer before college, and you ruined it. You ruined everything."

I was shaking so hard now that I couldn't even fight Sylvia off. Her arms wrapped around my shoulders, pulling me to her chest. "Shh... It's okay."

How could she stand me? I'd just bitched at my dad for marrying her, basically. For putting her and her kids first. She should have called me a brat. Or at least left the room.

But instead she hugged me. Kissed my hair, even. Like a mom. Like someone who cared. And I knew that she was like Nathan. She'd been there the whole time. That was why she annoyed me so much. It was because she was being a parent.

A heavy hand rested on my shoulder. "Munchkin," Dad murmured. "I . . . I am really sorry. I had no idea you felt this way." He paused, gently pulling me out of Sylvia's arms and turning me to face him. "Listen to me. I love you. You are my family, and I love you more than anything." He shook his head. "I guess your mother and I just got so caught up that we didn't realize we were taking you for granted."

"How come you never said anything?" I asked. "When the people on Facebook were calling me a slut, why didn't you ask me about it? Even Sylvia, who barely knew me, talked to me about it. Punish me, yell at me, be unreasonable. Why didn't you just do *something*?"

"Because I was scared of pushing you away. But I think I did that anyway." He looked at Sylvia, standing behind me. "Can I talk to Whitley? Alone."

I heard Sylvia let out a long sigh. "It's about time."

30

"I assume your mother told you why we got divorced," Dad said, sitting down next to me on the foot of his bed. "If she's still angry about it."

I shook my head. "No. She complained about you a lot, but she never told me about the cheating. Trace did."

Dad's head dropped. "One of my biggest regrets is that Trace got caught in the middle of all that. You were young enough to be kept in the dark, but Trace... We haven't been very close since he left, and I know that's why." Dad ran a hand through his hair. "I was a bad husband. It's my fault our family split up."

"Yeah," I said. "I know."

"I haven't been a great dad, either," he said. "Even after the divorce... I shouldn't have let you do the summer visits. I should have come to visit you or made you come see me more often. Then, when you did visit...I didn't see it then, but I realize now that I was more of a brother to you than a dad. I let you drink and told you stories and let you be around women I barely knew —"

"It wasn't so bad."

"Yes, it was," he said. "I was supposed to be your father. Not your best friend. But I'd been your friend for so long that I was scared to be your dad. When those pictures started popping up, and you lied about that party the night Bailey got drunk, I didn't know how to deal with it. I've been your buddy for so long, I didn't have the tools to know how to be your father. I hoped you'd get on by yourself or that you'd talk to Sylvia about it. I know, that's so wrong, but parents make idiotic mistakes sometimes, too."

"Why was the picture with Nathan different?" I asked.

Dad leaned forward, burying his face in his hands. He took a deep breath, then looked up at the ceiling before letting it out. "I broke up our family. So this time, when I was finally ready to settle down again, I didn't want anything to put it at risk. I just thought...with you and Nathan...the things people would say — it wouldn't just make the family look bad, it could hurt it, too."

"You don't think I know that?" He met my gaze. "Dad, I love the Caulfields. They've made me feel like I'm part of their family when my real family didn't feel like one anymore, and I love them for that. I know that Nathan and I seeing each other could cause problems down the road, if we split up or something. He knows that, too. But we can handle it."

"You think you can now, but —"

I shook my head. "We *can*. It might be tough, but we're adults now. It's our decision. And we're going to keep seeing each other at college, no matter what."

Dad didn't say anything for a long moment. Then he asked, "Do you really love him?"

"I...I think I'm getting close. I've never felt this way about anyone before."

"He's a good kid. I know he's had some issues in the past, but his heart's in the right place. And he feels the same way about you?"

I nodded. "No one in my life has cared about me the way he does."

"I don't know how to deal with this," he said. "I don't know how to be a dad or a stepdad or a husband. I'm trying, but I just keep screwing it up. I want everything to be so perfect this time."

"I know."

He reached out and wrapped an arm around my shoulder, pulling me toward him. "I'm sorry."

"I know."

"So, what do we do now?" he asked. "I don't know how to fix this. Tell me what to do."

"Don't make me go back to Mom's early," I said.

"I won't. What else?"

"Well..." I hesitated. "I don't know, either. I haven't felt

280

like part of a family in a long time, so this is weird for me, too. But we'll figure it out eventually."

A little while later, when I walked upstairs, I found my bedroom door unlocked and Nathan sitting on the floor looking at photos.

"You dressed up like Princess Leia for Halloween?" he asked. "I'm liking you more every day."

"What?" I knelt down beside him and saw that the photos he was looking at were of me. "Oh, yeah, that's from when I was eleven — the year before the divorce. Dad managed to convince me that Princess Leia was the coolest costume in the store — cooler than a ballerina dress, anyway. Where did you find this?"

"In the closet, with the rest of these," he said.

"These were in the closet?" I said, picking up another photo from the pile spread on the floor. It was of Dad and me fishing on Kentucky Lake two years ago, me sporting a sunburn almost as bad as the one I'd gotten this summer. "Wow. I always just assumed it was storage."

"You've never been in the closet?" he asked.

"No — but I'm wondering why *you* were in my closet."

He shrugged. "I got bored while you were downstairs. Did everything go okay?"

"Yeah," I said. "I'm not going back early. I don't know about the rest of the stuff yet, but it's all...*out there* now, I guess."

"Good." Nathan kissed me once, then picked up another photo. "You were a cute kid."

"I was lanky and awkward. Until I turned fifteen — then I got boobs." I stood up and walked over to the closet doors. "What else is in here?"

"Just some crazy-looking paintings."

"Oh my God," I said, staring at the psychedelic, colorful paintings leaned up against the wall of the closet. They were the ones from Dad's condo. I leaned forward to read the sticky note attached to the frame of the closest one.

Hi, Whitley!

I found these when we were unpacking and your dad thought you might want them. There are also some photographs in here that I found in a box. Feel free to decorate the room however you like. Can't wait to finally meet you!

Sylvia

I'd always imagined an ironing board or extra sheets in this closet. I'd never imagined this, never imagined things that belonged to me.

But this room had been mine all along.

"Hey, Nathan?"

"Hmm?"

"Do you know where I can get some nails and a hammer?"

"Uh, maybe. Why?"

I picked up the brightly colored abstract and carried it

into the middle of my room, standing it in front of Nathan. "Because," I said when he looked up at me. "I have a project for us."

"Looks good, munchkin."

I turned and found Dad standing in the doorway. "Thanks," I said, handing a nail up to Nathan, who was standing on the chair, so he could hang the last painting. "We're almost done."

"I haven't seen this picture in so long," he said, picking up the frame I'd put on my dresser. "This was taken — what? Ten years ago?"

"Something like that," I said. "I was eight, I think. My first basketball game at UK. Mom didn't want to go."

"That was a good day."

I nodded.

"Done," Nathan said, stepping down from the chair. "The decorating is complete."

I smiled, looking around my room. I may have only been staying there for another week or so, but I'd be back. And when I came back, this space would still be mine. No matter what.

"Hey, guys," Bailey said, poking her head through the doorway. "Mom wanted me to tell you dinner is ready."

"Good, because I'm starved," Nathan said, walking out the door.

"Me, too," Dad said, following after him. "Seriously, munchkin, the room looks great."

Bailey walked inside and looked around the room. "These paintings are weird."

"I know," I said. "But I like them."

She smiled at me. "I'm glad you're not leaving yet."

"Thanks," I said, walking into the hallway and down the stairs with her. "I'm glad, too."

31

"All right," Harrison said, stepping away from the fire. "Let's burn those little bitches."

"I still can't believe we're doing this," I said, handing him the pair of flip-flops I'd been wearing the night we met. "It's not like I've worn them since you told me they sucked."

"It's meant to be more of a symbolic thing than a prevention technique," he said, tossing the first shoe on the flames.

It was the next Thursday, the night before I was supposed to go back to Indiana. Harrison and I had taken Bailey shopping for clothes that morning. We'd spent hours at the mall in Oak Hill, letting her try on everything she wanted.

"You're going to knock 'em dead at school on Monday," Harrison told her in the checkout line. "The kids at Hamilton High won't know what hit them."

When we dropped her off at the house, we picked up

Nathan and headed out to Harrison's. He'd asked the two of us to sleep over. He'd invited Bailey, too, but she had an all-day cheer camp — a program to prep the new freshman cheerleaders — the next day. But Nathan and I said yes. It would be one last hurrah before I went back to Mom's and Harrison left for California. And he'd asked me to bring "those goddamn flip-flops."

Apparently, we were having a ceremonial burning.

Once he'd thrown the second shoe into the fire, he took a seat in the grass beside me. Nathan knelt a few feet away, fooling with the ancient cordless radio Harrison had dragged out to his backyard for us.

"So, when do you two move into your dorms?" Harrison asked.

"Monday," I said. "The same day Bailey starts high school."

"Who's taking you?"

"My mom."

"What about you, Nathan?"

"Mom and Greg," he said. "Aunt Sherri's taking Bailey to school."

"Uh-oh," Harrison said, looking at me. "Both your parents on campus? Think they'll run into each other?"

"Maybe."

I hadn't talked to Mom yet. Not since the fight where I'd called her self-absorbed. But Dad promised me that we'd both sit down with her tomorrow, when he took me back to Indiana. Yes, it was going to be awkward and uncomfortable, but it had been six years since the divorce. It was about time we worked things out. And we were going to do it together.

"So, have you figured out a major yet?" he asked. "Is it Russian? Please pick Russian."

I shook my head. "Nope. Still haven't picked."

"So what are you going to do?"

"I think I'll just be undeclared for a while," I said. "I'll take a class in everything that sounds interesting. Figure out what makes me happy. Even if I waste a year or two and have to stay in school longer, I think it'll be worth it to find something I love."

"But you're going to take Russian, right?" he asked. "Just one class."

I laughed. "We'll see."

"When do you start classes, Harrison?" Nathan asked.

"Week from Monday," he said. "Mom and I are flying out to L.A. the Friday before to check out the area. I think she's more excited than I am. Speaking of which" — he got to his feet —"I'd better go tell her good night, or she'll be out here in half an hour doing her best to embarrass me. Be right back."

I watched him run up to his back door, smiling to myself. I'd been so resistant to having a best friend again, but Harrison had forced himself into my life. I was going to miss him so much. But we'd call and text and maybe, if he talked me into it, I'd even get on Facebook. One thing was for sure — I wasn't going to let Harrison go easily. And I hoped he wouldn't let me go, either.

"Finally," Nathan said as he located a radio station that played clearly. He scooted over to sit next to me. We were both in shorts, and my bare knee leaned against his as we watched the last shreds of my flip-flops being devoured by the flames, stinking up the delicious smell of the wood fire with burning rubber. "So," he said. "Are you ready to go home tomorrow?"

"I'm not going home," I said, shaking my head. "This place is my home. Despite all the shit that went down this summer, it's my home, more than my mom's house has ever been."

"So . . . the answer is no, then."

"I guess." I leaned back on my elbows, stretching my feet out in front of me. "But I'm ready to start school. Even though I have no idea what I'm doing. I'm ready to start figuring myself out, you know?"

"Yeah. I know."

We sat in silence for a while, just listening to the fire crackle and the radio sing. Then the song faded away, and it was replaced by another.

"Hey," Nathan said, brightening up.

"Yeah. Van Morrison."

"It's 'Brown Eyed Girl.' Our song."

I rolled my eyes. "Nathan, this is not our song."

"Fine. What is our song, then?"

"Easy. It's 'Wonderwall.'"

"Wonder-what?"

I glared at him. "You're kidding, right? 'Wonderwall'! It's by Oasis. One of the biggest hits of the nineties. One of the greatest songs of all time?" When no recognition dawned on his face, I opened my mouth to sing it, but Nathan leaned down and put a hand over my mouth.

"Stop. You can't sing."

I batted his hand away. "Shut up. You're a jerk."

"Why is that our song?" he asked, laughing.

"Because it's a classic and it's deep — at least in a they-were-probably-high-when-they-wrote-it sort of way — and it's one of my favorites and it has nothing to do with brown eyes. So 'Wonderwall' is our song. Deal with it."

"Whatever you say." He leaned down and kissed me. It was meant to be just a quick peck, but I turned, pushing my weight down on my left elbow and wrapping my other arm around his neck, twisting my fingers in his soft, dark hair.

"We are going to have so much fun at college together," I breathed against his lips.

"Oh yeah?" he asked, pulling away just an inch. "You think you'll come to a basketball game? Watch me warm up the bench once in a while?"

"Only if you'll join me under the bleachers a few times," I said.

"I might."

He leaned in to kiss me again, but Harrison's shout of "Get a room, you two!" convinced him to pull back.

Harrison came hurrying out of his house, three large

bundles in his arms. "Here you go," he said, dropping one beside me.

"What's this?"

"A sleeping bag."

"We're sleeping out here tonight?" Nathan asked, taking one of the other bundles from Harrison.

"Yep."

"Why?" I asked.

"Because it's the last night of our summer together," he said, unfurling his bundle in the grass beside me. "And it's fucking beautiful out here, so why not?"

Nathan and I spread out our own sleeping bags. I was in the middle, the boys lying close on either side of me. We talked for a long time, laughing, staring up at the stars, making plans for the future when we'd meet up again. After an hour or so, the boys fell asleep, leaving me in silence.

I wished that moment didn't have to end. A gorgeous summer night with my best friend and my first boyfriend. It was perfect. And I was *happy*.

But there would be other perfect moments, more friends, more times to be happy — they might not come easy, but they'd come. And no matter what, no matter what ups and downs and ins and outs I faced, I had a family I could turn to. One that would love me unconditionally. It felt good to know that again.

I closed my eyes and nestled down into my sleeping bag. Tomorrow, seeing Mom, would be tough. But I'd get through it. Then, a few days later, I'd get to start over in a new place, with new people, with no reputation or rumors. No hiding, no wallowing, no begging for my parents to notice me. Just a chance to start over and figure out exactly who it was I wanted to be.

Screw nightmares. I was waking up.

ACKNOWLEDGMENTS

First and foremost, I have to thank my family. My parents, grandparents, siblings, aunts, uncles, cousins — you have all shown your support and confidence in me. Thank you so much for loving me and making Whitley's loneliness a complete work of imagination.

Enormous gratitude also goes to the women who make my dreams come true. To Joanna Volpe, who loved this book way before I did — thank you, Jo, for your undying faith in me, even when I don't always have faith in myself. And, as always, this book would not exist if it weren't for Kate Sullivan, who loved Whitley at her worst and helped me find her best. You two never let me down.

Thanks also to Cindy Eagan, Lisa Sabater, Tracy Shaw, JoAnna Kremer, Stacy Abrams, and the team over at Little,

Brown. You guys never cease to amaze me! Also, Nancy Coffey and Sara Kendall, who are, in general, fabulous.

Love and appreciation also go to my friends. There are too many of you to name here, but you know who you are. Special thanks go to Loretta Nyhan, Holly Bodger, Lee Bross, Amanda Hannah, Courtney Allison Moulton, and Amy Lukavics, who all helped shape this story in some way, or shaped me as a writer. I couldn't do this without you all. And thanks, of course, to the girls at YA Highway. I love you guys so much.

And last — but never, ever least — thanks to my readers. You are the reason I write, the reason this job is my dream. Thank you for letting my characters into your hearts.